THE SUN IS
ALWAYS SHINING

Letreece,

Let your light shine!

Love DJ!

THE SUN IS ALWAYS SHINING

A Story of Adversity Turned to Triumph

DeAntwann Johnson

Library of Congress Control Number:		2017916774
ISBN:	Hardcover	978-1-5434-6232-6
	Softcover	978-1-5434-6233-3
	eBook	978-1-5434-6234-0

Print information available on the last page.
Originally Edited by Charlene E. Green
Cover Designed by Ebony Miles
Author Photo by Cherrelle Avery, Shades of Film Photography

www.djinspires.com

Rev. date: 11/28/2017

To order additional copies of this book, contact:
Xlibris
1-888-795-4274
www.Xlibris.com
Orders@Xlibris.com
765725

DEDICATION

"This book is dedicated, first and foremost, to Britney and Makai. To my siblings who have always looked to me as their leader, failing to realize that my strength comes from them. To my family members who have had a hand in me being the man I am today. To my mother and father, and everyone else I have adopted as mother and father. And lastly, Mr. Hines. Words can't express how much you have meant to my life. Thank You!"

CONTENTS

CHAPTER 1

The Beginning

It was a storm from the beginning. In a small city in Indiana, my sixteen-year-old mother—a child herself—was about to bring a child into this world. She was so nervous about the possibility of being pregnant again. She was pregnant one other time, when she was thirteen years old, and her mother forced her to abort the baby. She feared her mom might just force her to get rid of another baby this time around.

She made sure to go to a place where she could check on her pregnancy without having to get permission from her mother. It was confirmed. She was pregnant for a second time, hopeful she would be able to keep this one. I'm not sure if my mom and dad were ready to embark on this journey, but they both were excited. My mom knew she had to tell my grandmother eventually and enlisted some help from her uncle. Anxious as a high-stakes blackjack player, she told her mom, who—to my mom's surprise—said that she knew. Mom breathed a sigh of relief that was like no other. She thought my grandmother was going to kill her, so this came as a big surprise. It was an acceptance that my mom hadn't felt in a long time.

The pregnancy was smooth all the way up until my birth on Monday, November 14, 1988. I didn't know how much of a miracle I was that day. When she was forced to abort the first baby, she didn't take it well but ultimately knew it was for the best. It wasn't her wish to give up the baby, but her life had been anything but normal.

To understand the idea of my life, we must analyze what the precursor to it was. My mother was living with her mom and her stepdad. She didn't have the slightest idea of what it meant to be a good mom; her mom was not a great example. She had not the slightest idea of what a good man looked like. She couldn't tell the difference between an impostor and one who loved her. A man in the family loved her and abused that love. She was molested, and that started the string of heartbreaking and unhappy years. My mother had no idea how to cope with the molestation or the abortion of her baby at thirteen. It must've been so tough to have to deal with those things back-to-back. She was forced to sweep both of those pains under the rug.

That seems to be the thing in some black families: they inherit hand-me-down slave mentalities—the idea of utilizing oppressive ideologies instilled in African American slaves hundreds of years ago. What goes on in the family stays in the family, and what is done in the dark stays in the dark. The only problem with that logic is that when you are forced to be with your broken heart and thoughts, you are already mentally destroying any semblance of hope—hope to live a life of prosperity and goodwill and to have a healthy mind, body, and spirit. It gets ripped from you like the native land before Columbus stepped foot on it, like many other unwanted changes. Then after you are broken down to the very being that you start to despise, slave mentality advises you not to see a therapist because God will handle your emotional ills.

My mother's spirit broke long before her water did. She was a kid who has pain no one could imagine, all alone until she met boys pretending to be men who could make her feel good. She was not going to allow her mother to make her abort this baby, not this time. Many people felt like she made a mistake by having me at sixteen, but she saw something that could make her crack even the slightest of smiles. It was destiny that I ended up being her eldest child—and a miracle that I wasn't another abortion. I don't know if it is meant for me to know why I was the one allowed to be born, but I thank God every day.

My father's story is different but similar. He had it rough growing up. His mother left him at a young age without any explanation, and he was forced to live with his abusive father. He eventually would stay with his grandma, who took him in as her own. However, that came with its fair share of struggles. His grandma had to take care of him along with six other boys. She didn't have much money to care for all of them, so they went hungry at times. One time they didn't have any food, so they ate popcorn for a week. Eventually, the poverty got too hard to deal with, so he turned to wicked ways. He decided that he would steal food. He would steal all the time to make sure they ate. He didn't do it because he wanted to have fun; he did it so he and his family could survive.

While he was in school, he got into trouble for fighting and talking back to authorities. At home, his dad would beat him and his brothers; but when he was fourteen, he reached his breaking point. One time his dad got so mad at him and his brother that he used jumper cables to whip them. My dad decided that he didn't want to experience that pain again, so he ran away and became a son of the streets. It was downhill from there.

When he met my mom, he was only with her, but that didn't last. When he found out she was pregnant, they were on and off with each other until it got close for me to be born. She found out that he was being unfaithful, which she didn't tolerate, so it put an end to their relationship. After the breakup, my dad stayed in town, but he wasn't around much.

When it was time for me to be born, my mother had to try everything under the sun to get me to come out. It seemed that I wasn't ready, or I just wanted to be born on a specific date. My mother had finally gone into labor and would remain so for fourteen hours. Her mom was not in the room with her, and my dad was not at the hospital when I was born (a preview of the type of father he would be to me as I grew up). The only person in the hospital room was my mother's aunt, and she ended up getting kicked out of the room because she was getting on my mother's nerves, so it was just my mother, the doctor, and the staff.

The doctor wanted to know if my mother wanted to watch me being born, and she said yes. So she watched intently through the mirror as she pushed out her miracle baby. As I got closer and closer to taking my first breath of air, she noticed my full head of black hair. She began to cry when I was finally out because she was so happy to have something she could love and to know, without a shadow of a doubt, that she would be loved back. My mom had so much love to give and didn't know what to do with it. She decided that she would give it all to me. She wouldn't even let the nurses touch me. The doctor asked for my name and my mom said, "Jeremy Deon Allen." Later, my grandma would also fall in love with me at first sight as did everyone else who met me.

My dad came to the hospital later when he found out that I had arrived. He was so happy to see me as I was his first child of what would be many. After my birth, he and my mother were not able to make their relationship work. My dad ended up dropping out of school, and my mother followed soon after. This would be the introduction of a life full of storms for both.

CHAPTER 2

Family

My mom was seventeen when she met my stepdad, Luther. He was a real charmer; he swept my mom off her feet with every word. It was enough to make her forget about any hurt she was dealing with after my dad. He was really good to me and my mom. He took good care of our family.

The first couple of years with my mom and stepdad went by fast. I was going on two years old when my sister Mercedes was born. Yes, she was named after the car. My stepdad loved cars. He wanted to name at least one of his kids after a car. Mercedes and I were pretty close. One of the few pictures that I remember of my childhood was a picture that I took with my sister, in which I had on a red Christmas sweater, red pants, and Nikes. My sister had on a pretty red dress, and we both were smiling.

The next year, my mother gave birth to my brother, Luther Jr. We called him Junior, and he looked just like my stepdad. We all were living in Fort Wayne, Indiana, in the Blue Waters Apartments. We were a happy family now. Nothing could tear us down.

My mother and stepdad eventually moved us to a house on Greenbriar Street. One day I was playing with something, and I broke it, and my mom summoned me to the upstairs bedroom. I was a nervous wreck, but at this time, I was receiving fairly minor whippings. My mom started whipping me, and I decided that I would be a tough guy and not cry. Well, my mother got fed up with that and summoned my stepdad to come and take over. I thought, *Man, I should've just pretended like my mom's whippings hurt.*

5

That was the first time I was whipped by my stepdad, and it certainly wouldn't be the last.

My siblings were still very young and didn't get into as much trouble as I did. We then moved to a house on Pineview Street, and this was when we started to experience a different side of my stepdad. By this time, my other sister Renee was born. This was also the time when I first started to notice that my stepdad was a heavy drinker. One day he called me up to their room and wanted me to try his Budweiser. It was the nastiest thing I had ever tried in my life. At that time, I was about five years old; and if he were trying to get me to not drink, then he accomplished his goal.

Later that week, he and my mother got into a big argument, and it was so bad that he ended up dragging my screaming mother up the stairs to our front door by her hair. It was the first time I heard my mom scream and cry, and it was the first time I felt helpless. We eventually moved to Wooden Cove Apartments, where the abuse to her and us kids continued, and then to Willowbrook Apartments, where the bulk of my childhood took place.

CHAPTER 3

Consequences

The Willowbrook Apartments ended up being the longest tenure we would ever have in any place when I lived with my mom and stepdad. In hindsight, I hoped that meant there would be stability and that this was a place where we could start to reverse the curses of our slave mentality. It was hope in a bottle. The only problem was the bottle was thrown into the Lake Michigan of my heart, never to be found.

It was a three-bedroom, one-bathroom townhome apartment. It was two stories with a playground behind our building and plenty of playing space in the front. My sisters shared a room, and I shared a room with my brother. We were never rich by any stretch of the imagination. We walked to places when we didn't have a car. We shopped at the cheapest grocery stores you can think of, and we rarely ate out or ordered pizza.

If there was one thing from my childhood that I cherish the most, it was my mother being the most amazing cook. I am a good cook today because she wouldn't kick me out of the kitchen. She grew up having to cook for family members all the time, and that really showed in her cooking. She was a veteran.

I navigated through kindergarten quickly at Watson/Sutton Elementary and was excited about 1st grade. The school had two names because it was set up for students to do kindergarten to second grade at Watson and third to fifth grade at Sutton. I was on my best behavior because I had wanted to go to school since I was old enough to talk. When I was younger, I often bugged my mom about going to school. I would get so excited when I saw a bus and kids going off to school, and I would ask her when I would be able to go. Her answer was "In due time."

I excelled in first grade. I seemed to be picking up things quickly. When I was home, we seemed to be the typical American family. My stepdad, Luther, was working one of his jobs. He was handy with cars. My mom would only work every now and then since she was a stay-at-home mom. She loved her soap operas. I believe she got that from my grandmother.

One thing I could never understand with my mom was why she would smoke cigarettes around us—all the time. In fact, there were times she would demand that I light her cigarette for her with the stove burner. She didn't know, or she at least pretended not to know, that I would take a puff or two just to see what it was like. It's a wonder that I didn't end up smoking when I got older. It was something I never understood, but back then, cigarettes were so cheap that they didn't make a big deal about how bad they were for you until later.

Things seemed to be normal around our household, and when things were normal, something was always bound to happen. I got in trouble for the first time in school when I called my first-grade teacher, Ms. Lake, fat. I am not sure why I did that, but I asked myself that question many times until I got home and faced the consequences.

When I arrived, I was told to go to my room and pull my pants down. There was no such thing as a whipping with clothes on. We almost always received whippings to our bare bottoms. I trembled in fear as I awaited what I knew was going to be a painful punishment. With every step Luther took up the stairs, my heart dropped into my stomach like a boulder. When he got upstairs, I could hear him grab his infamous brown leather belt, and then he proceeded to question why I did what I did. I had no explanation, and the whipping ensued. It seemed like it lasted awhile, and I cried so loud that I'm sure my neighbors could hear me. (It amazes me how much my neighbors heard and didn't bother to check and see if people were okay as the years progressed.)

A sigh of relief crept in as he finished and said his last words, which usually consisted in cursing and strong sentiments that ingrained in us that he was in charge and we should fear him, and then he left me in the room with my tears. I took it easy as I sat on my bed; my booty was so sore.

My mom seemed to be helpless when it came to defending us from my stepfather. In fact, they argued a lot about how abusive he was with us. It was a battle that she was not going to win. They also argued about him coming home at all hours of the night; sometimes he would leave home for days at a time.

I was convinced that my stepfather was only concerned about himself. One of the things he did was use the restroom for a long time, with no regard for anyone else in the house. There was one time when Luther was in the bathroom doing number two (having a bowel movement), and I had to use the restroom so bad that I could barely hold it. Every time he was in there, he took an extremely long time as if no one else's bathroom needs mattered. I was so afraid of asking him if I could use the restroom that I ended up crapping my pants. It was so embarrassing. The most messed-up part about it was that had he found out, I would've been beaten down. I ended up cleaning myself up the best I could and hiding my clothes in the closet.

At that time, I didn't realize how messed up it was to not be able to use the restroom. It's something that everyone deserves, and I was not given that essential right. All I knew was my fear of my stepdad was deep, and I didn't want to get in the way of him. That meant peace for me, and I was intent on staying peaceful, even if it meant crapping my pants.

A couple of months later, it was quiet and normal around the home. The definition of *normal* changed dramatically. My seventh birthday was here, and it was a great celebration. One of the gifts was a watch that Luther and Mom got me. Luther had been bragging to his friend, who was visiting, about how smart I was and how proud of me he was. He tested me to see if I could tell time, to show the friend how advanced I was for a first grader, but I couldn't tell the time because it was in a different function. He looked at the watch and changed the function for me, and I rattled off the time with ease. That was the first time he was proud to call me his son. At that point in my life, I didn't really know my biological dad, so I grew up thinking that Luther was my real dad; and at times like this, I didn't mind calling him my dad.

Mom often took us grocery shopping with her. We mainly only got the essentials, so we weren't able to eat out. As big as our family was, we went through food quickly, so Mom was always cooking.

One time I went to the store with her, and for whatever reason, I wanted some baseball cards I saw. I put the cards in my pocket and tried to walk out unnoticed, but my mom spotted me and had me confess to the security guard that I stole them. I had to put them back, and I was embarrassed. I am not sure why I got that urge, but I wanted those cards. I cried because my mom said I may get arrested. I can't say that method of punishment worked because I didn't stop stealing until I was a teenager. To this day, I'm not sure how the heck I picked up that habit.

CHAPTER 4

Pain

A few months later, my thoughts of Luther being a good dad went down the drain as his drinking got the best of him. One day he was really drunk outside with neighbors, having a good time but ultimately causing a ruckus. My mother attempted to try to get him to come into the house, and he did not like that. He slapped her in front of all our neighbors. As if that weren't enough, he attempted to slap her again, and she ran away from him. He chased her around the parking lot as she pleaded for him to stop and calm down. Once again, our neighbors seemed to really believe they should mind their business because they didn't try to intervene.

My mom eventually made her way into the house, where Luther was trying to get in as well. He finally calmed down, and she let him in. As soon as he walked in, he punched her in the face and called her a bitch. She began to wail, and that was the second time I felt helpless because I was powerless against this man who stood at six feet three inches and weighed two-hundred-plus pounds. He was a guy who committed to lifting weights in his day.

I felt angry because that was my mother down there taking a beating, and I wasn't able to do anything about it. What I could do was comfort my siblings, who were equally scared. That was the first time I had thoughts of killing Luther. There I was, young and afraid, thinking about how I would end his life. Would I get a knife from the kitchen and stab him in his sleep? My anger and frustration in that moment had me thinking all types of evil ideas.

When Luther went to work the next day, my mom decided she couldn't take the abuse anymore, and we went to stay in a women's shelter, which was a welcoming sight. We had all our needs met. They had a playroom, TV room, comfortable beds, and good food. We also got all the toiletries you could think of. I didn't realize how low our income was until we stayed at the women's shelter. As a kid, I had no idea what was rich and what was poor. All I knew was that I had family that sometimes fought, but at the end of the day, we had one another.

While we were at the shelter, I was excited that we weren't in harm's way. My mom was miserable. It had something to do with having to rely on other people to provide for her kids. I also think that she ultimately missed Luther. She would call him, and he would beg her to come home. We were safe in the shelter because they had a tight security system in place. They didn't allow just any person in, which made sense because most of the women were running from their abusers.

I still went to school, and it was just like I was going to school from home except that I was safer, and now there was no threat from Luther. A week had passed, and my mother decided she'd had enough. She didn't like all the rules they had at the shelter and decided to go back home but under certain conditions. I believe Luther would've said anything to get his way. That was what he was known for—hurting and deceiving people.

When we returned home, things seemed to go pretty smooth. In fact, for their anniversary, Luther and my mom went away and left us with a babysitter who lived a couple of apartments down. The babysitter was a young lady who was fresh out of high school, and she had a sister who was in middle school. I was still in first grade at the time.

Whenever we were alone, the younger sister would always want to do sexual things with me. At the time, I didn't think of it as abuse; I looked at it as being cool that this older girl wanted to do those things with me. I thought I knew about sex; when my mother and Luther had sex, she was very loud. I thought that this girl didn't mean any harm. Even when everyone wanted to go outside and play, including me, the girl would force me to stay inside and participate in sexual activities with her.

The day before my parents came back from their trip, she wanted me to lie down while she gave me oral sex. It tickled, so I didn't want her to do it. She got upset, threatened to tell her boyfriend on me, and then left. Later that week, her boyfriend took my bike and threw it in the trash can. That pissed me off because I felt I hadn't done anything wrong. His girl seduced me, and I was only in first grade.

My parents returned from the trip and seemed to be in good spirits. Although my mom did cook often, Luther had set a precedence that would only allow us to eat when the food was ready, not necessarily when we were hungry. We were afraid to do a lot of things, afraid to make even the slightest amount of noise. When we were thirsty, we would make our hands into a cup and drink from the bathroom sink; and if we were *really* thirsty, we would drink water from our shoes.

After dinner, I was always tasked with doing dishes. If there was one dish that wasn't clean enough, Luther would take out every single dish, and I would have to wash them. I was up until the wee hours of the night cleaning those dishes, hoping and wishing I cleaned them to his satisfaction. I was finally allowed to go to bed, and he mumbled something like, "I bet he don't leave a dirty dish on the counter next time." I walked up to my room while cursing him in my mind.

CHAPTER 5

Slave?

In 1996, my youngest sister, Lexus, was born. This was the summer before my eighth birthday. While my mother was in the hospital, we were alone at home with Luther. We dreaded being alone with him because we were on pins and needles all the time. It was like being in jail or a detention center. We could not make a peep and were at the mercy of his ways. When one of my siblings would make too much noise, he would hold me responsible.

One time, when my siblings came down to eat their dinner, they were served a hot meal, and he served me slices of Wonder Bread and water. I was punished often for the mishaps of my siblings, and I couldn't figure out why. I just tried to keep them in line, and it really contributed to my having to do things that kids aren't supposed to be doing. I was a child taking care of other children. I was aware that this was an adult job, not one for a person of my age. I felt like I wasn't allowed to be a kid. And if I didn't make sure my siblings stayed in line, I would get in trouble.

My mother had finally come home with my little sister, and things were back to normal—*normal* meaning nonchaotic. Even though the abuse from Luther was still in effect, there was something about having Mom around during those times that gave me comfort. I felt like as long as she was there when Luther would fly into a rage, at least there was a chance that she could stop him. When we were alone with him, there was less chance that we would be able to avoid his wrath.

In fall of that same year, on a Sunday, I was hungry, and my mother was running errands. Luther had instilled such fear in me that I didn't want to tell him I was hungry; I just tried to wait until it was time to eat. My little sister Lexus had a Pop-Tart in her crib that she was not eating. I grabbed a piece of it and ate it. Thirty minutes later, my mom had returned and was getting dinner ready. I was in my room when Luther came in, looking angry, and punched me in the face. I immediately screamed because the pain was so sudden. My eye began to swell quickly. He shouted, "Don't you ever take food from your little sister!"

My mom ran upstairs to see what all the commotion was, and he pushed past her. She consoled me and told me that everything was going to be all right. She went back to confront Luther, who was showing no remorse. Luckily, he didn't hit her, but he did return to my room to threaten me if I told anyone. I wondered how I was going to explain things when I went to school so I wouldn't be hurt again by him.

The next day, my eye was black, and I could barely see out of it. When I got to school on Monday, everyone was looking at me and wondering what happened to me. I was sent to the office by the teacher. When I got to the office, I was met with questions about who hurt me and if I was okay. I told them I was jumped by a group of sixth graders. For some reason, they accepted that as truth, gave me some ice, and sent me on my way. The idea of those people in that office not probing me further about things made me wonder if Luther was invincible. Would he continue to get away with terrorizing our family forever?

Luther's terror would hit its apex at the end of my second-grade year. It was the last day of school, and everyone was excited, including me. At Watson/Sutton, we finished second grade at one school and attended third grade at a different school. It had the same feeling when people moved from elementary to middle school or from middle to high school.

All the second graders were slated to watch a movie, and I had to sit out the first five to ten minutes because of a minor violation. I can't remember what exactly (I was a frequent troublemaker), but it was small enough that it didn't cause me to miss the whole movie. While I was walking back to the other class, a student who often picked on me laughed and made fun of me because I wasn't allowed to watch the movie. I yelled at him to shut up, and the teacher who was in the vicinity felt that was grounds for me to be sent to the office. Anytime I was sent to the office, I begged and pleaded for them not to send me there, to no avail.

They called my home, and it just so happened that Luther was the only person there; my mom was out running errands. He came up to the school to pick me up, and it was silent all the way home. Thoughts were running through my mind about what was going to happen. *Am I going to receive the worst whipping ever?* I wasn't sure, but I would get my answer soon enough. When we got home, he told me to go upstairs and get ready. That meant I needed to be naked and ready to receive my whipping.

To make things better for me, I got the bright idea to hide the belt, thinking that he would not whip me since he couldn't find it. Boy, was I wrong. He knew that I hid the belt, and he laughed because he had a great replacement in mind—an extension cord. As he laughed his way to my room, I braced myself. Nothing could prepare me for what was coming next. As he began to whip me with the extension cord, I cried so loud that there was no way my neighbors could not hear. But they never bothered to check. The pain of the extension cord on my back was something I had never felt before and have not felt since. It literally ripped my skin open; it was as if he were my master and I were his slave.

I blacked out during the next three or four minutes. I woke up when it was all finished, and I lay there naked, unable to do anything with my back as it was tender and painful. It also left welt marks on my lower back that can still be seen today. It was a moment that left me in a deep dark place. I didn't want to continue to experience this pain. I didn't believe that life was worth living. I wanted to die in the worst way. If living was this painful, then I didn't want any part of it.

I didn't tell my mother when she got home. At this point, I felt like she couldn't do anything anyway. But she did find out. The next day, we were at the community center my aunt Faye owned. It was a house that was converted into an after-school center for kids, and it had a basement that functioned as a makeshift Goodwill store. While the kids played outside, the adults had adult conversation in the center.

I was playing with the other kids, and my shirt lifted for a moment. Aunt Faye saw my back and doubled over in fear, asking my mother what was wrong with my back. My mom was confused and didn't know what was going on. She pulled my shirt up, and the wounds on my back looked like they were fresh from a master's beating. She got upset and asked who did it. At first, I wouldn't say anything. She asked again. I told her it was Luther. I am not sure if she didn't know or she didn't want to believe that he did it, but I was taken aback when she was mad at me for not telling her what happened sooner.

To this day, I am not sure why she got so mad, considering that she didn't have much luck trying to prevent him from doing the things he had done to me and my siblings. My siblings would get whippings, but I took the brunt of all of it. My aunt began to express her concerns about this, and all my mother could say was "Yeah, yeah." I got some ointment put on my back and went back to playing, as kids do, not feeling any need to wallow in self-pity.

CHAPTER 6

Darkness

I always wondered if Luther would meet his match. I daydreamed about someone really challenging him, but as I mentioned before, I was beginning to think he was invincible. It turns out he wasn't; he was finally arrested for domestic abuse charges. Another argument turned ugly. This time, he left my mother with a black eye and a busted lip. I could hear her sobbing as she lay on the floor, with him towering her.

I guess the neighbors finally had enough of the screaming and crying because they called the police. My mother did not want to press charges, but Luther could not get out of this one. Off to jail he went, and all I could do was breathe a sigh of relief. As I went downstairs to console my mother, I could sense that she had been battered to the point where it seemed she was losing her sense of self.

My mother did her best after that. With the breadwinner being locked away, we really tried to make ends meet. It was tough at first. A few weeks later, my mom wasn't able to get enough money together to keep the lights on, and we had to be in the dark. My mom made the most out of the situation and would tell us scary stories by candlelight. Once we were able to get the lights back on, it seemed that everything was smooth, but I always sensed that my mother felt alone. I don't know what it was that made her want to be with a man who was so bad for her, and she went into deep depression. The pressure of having to take care of five kids by herself while her husband was in jail for abusing her led to a breaking point.

One night my siblings and I were downstairs watching television while my mother was upstairs. We were watching *Space Jam*. My mother yelled downstairs for me and gave me instructions to finish the movie and go to our next-door neighbor's house. At first, I didn't think anything of it; I was fresh out of second grade. I asked her if we could get cookies and juice while we watched the movie, and she gave us permission.

As the movie was nearing the end, I started to get curious about why my mom would want us to go to the neighbor's house. I yelled upstairs to let my mom know that the movie was over. She didn't answer. I yelled again, "Mom, the movie is over!" No answer again. Then I walked up the stairs and knocked on the door. Again, no answer.

I went downstairs to get my siblings and bring them to the neighbor's house a couple of apartments away. She was one of the few neighbors we had a decent relationship with. She opened the door and wondered why we were at her house so late at night. I told her that my mother instructed us to come over. Surprised, she took us in and immediately went to our apartment to see what was going on. She came back panicked and asked her son to call the police.

The police and ambulance arrived, and they had to break down the door to her room. My mother attempted to commit suicide by overdosing on prescription and over-the-counter drugs. If I had not gone when I did, it could've been another traumatic event that I would've had to get through.

As Mom was rushed to the hospital, the neighbors called our family members, and we ended up staying with my aunt Brenda for a couple of days. I enjoyed myself while staying at my aunt's house. She loved video games, and it was like we were at an arcade in her house. That was the first time I played Super Nintendo. *Street Fighter* was the game of choice, and my favorite fighter to fight with was Ryu because he would say "hadoken" whenever he shot a fireball. I thought he said, "Awoo-shit!" My aunt thought it was funny, but she told me not to say it again.

After my mother was recovered and out of the hospital, she came to bring us back to our Willowbrook apartment. Two weeks had passed, and my maternal grandmother, Paris, felt it was necessary for my mother to get away from it all and take a vacation. The family had planned to go to Panama City, Florida, and they had an extra ticket, and they wanted her to go with them. My mom couldn't get anyone to come and babysit on such short notice, so they came up with the bright idea to leave us home by ourselves, and a lady would come and check in on us every so often. Lexus was the only one who stayed at the actual babysitter's apartment, which was in a different building from ours, while the rest of us—Mercedes, Luther Jr., Renee, and I—stayed in our apartment.

In all the excitement of getting away for a few days, Mom left in a hurry, and we were left to tear up the house. This was the summer after my second-grade year, and I was the oldest. I was so excited that we had an apartment all to ourselves. So many things went wrong. I am surprised we didn't get the police called on us for making so much noise. With this newfound freedom, we found ways to get into ample trouble. One time we put Pine-Sol in the fan and turned it on, which should've probably blown it up, but it didn't. We left a mop bucket with so much dirt in it that maggots started to hatch in it.

The babysitter checked in but not as much as she should've. One thing I have realized, looking back, is there was a lot of turning the other cheek happening in those apartments. When do you feel the need to say something? When does your heart take over and tell you to do something? It was so rare that people in our environment took action to help us, and it was really upsetting.

My mom eventually returned from her trip, and she had the *audacity* to be upset when she returned to a pretty messy apartment. Granted, we didn't mess it up as much as we could have, but she wasn't happy. I don't know what she was expecting when she came back since she left us in the house alone. She was lucky we weren't gone when she got back. We ended up helping her get the house in order, and everything was back to where it needed to be.

In my neighborhood, I befriended Christian, a Mexican kid, who was going to the third grade like I was. We played outside until we had to come in. He also invited me into his home. It was so nice to be able to go to a place where I could be safe. We became such good friends that his mother used to let me stay the night at their house. The first time I stayed the night, which was a first at a nonrelative's home, we played Super Nintendo until the wee hours of the night and then finally fell asleep.

The next day, we ate breakfast that his mother made. His stepdad ended up taking us fishing, which I had never done before. It was refreshing being treated the way they treated me. With them, I didn't feel like an outcast, like I did in my own home. After fishing, I tried to hang out with him as much as I could. One time I wanted to be out of the house so bad that I went over to his house when he wasn't home. Instead of going home, I lay on the couch that they had left outside their apartment, hoping they would return soon so I would be able to hang out with them for as long as possible instead of going home right away. It was close to noon, and I ended up falling asleep. When I woke up and they still weren't back, I got up and went home disappointed.

Every time my friend was home, when he wasn't visiting his dad, I went over to hang out with him. I never invited people over to my home because I didn't feel comfortable, even though Luther was still in jail. One day I was hanging with Christian and I saw that he had a jar of change in his living room. We didn't have much, and I would always want to get candy or snacks from the candy man with a colorful van and who would come through our apartments constantly. I got the urge to take some change and put it in my pocket.

When I left his house to head home, Christian must've noticed. He chased me, took me down, and took the change back. He yelled at me to never come back to his home again. He looked at me in disgust and disappointment. I was embarrassed and instantly felt sorry. I had never been confronted like that, and I ended up losing a true friend. I eventually made amends by going to his house and apologizing to him and his family, promising that it would never happen again. I understood if they didn't let me in their house again. We did become friends again, and I didn't do anything else to jeopardize our friendship.

One night when I returned home late from hanging with Christian, my mom had been yelling my middle name really loud for me to come home. As I started to walk up, she looked like she was going to whip me. This would've been normal, but she was going to do it in front of all my friends who lived in the apartment building with us. I didn't want that embarrassment, so I started to run away from her. I ran for a while through the apartment complex, which had about twenty buildings, until I reached the very back of our apartments, where my mom and her friend cornered me, and I started to climb a baseball fence. I stayed up there for another ten minutes before I was finally forced down, and the long walk back to our apartment ensued. When we made it home, I figured I would get a terrible whipping, but my mom said she was so mad that she couldn't whip me that night and would do it in the morning. That whipping never came, thank goodness.

While Luther was in jail, we went outside and played a lot more. I got into my first fight in front of our apartment when a boy was picking on my brother. Well, I wouldn't call it a fight. I didn't want to fight the kid, so I threw him down on the ground, pinned him down, and told him to leave me and my family alone, or I would beat him up next time. He agreed, I let him up, and he walked away and left my family alone.

I also got my first girlfriend during this time. We were both starting third grade soon. She was pretty, and she had two elder sisters. She was so smart. I knew I had a winner. We would call each other boyfriend and girlfriend until one day she broke up with me to be with another kid who was in our grade. When I found out, I was so upset and angry that I confronted him, and we ended up fighting.

This was the time I was starting to see my attitude take a turn for the worse, but who could blame me? A lot of frustration had built up in me when Luther was torturing our family. I didn't have the proper outlets to combat this anger, and I was fiery because of it. Despite having this anger issue, I was really starting to enjoy my childhood a little more. It would be a couple of months before Luther's unwanted return. When he came back, it seemed that he was somewhat rehabilitated. I'd be lying if I said he wasn't up to his abusive ways.

I was now in the third grade with Ms. Clarkson, one of my all-time favorite teachers. I am not sure why I liked her so much, but it was partly because she was pretty and black. When you live in a city that is predominantly white, you notice when people of color are in positions of power.

We also had a black principal. I spent many times in her office. One day I was playing around in the cafeteria, and she scolded me and threatened to pop me in the head with a can of soda. Of course, I went home and told my mom. She called to speak to the principal about it, but she denied it. I was in the office so often that I would memorize the old maze screensaver they had on the computers back in the day. That thing was so addictive.

Ms. Clarkson was as real as they came. She told me how it was, and I think I liked her so much because she wasn't so quick to call me to the office like my other teachers. She gave me many chances before I was sent to the office. I continued to be a good student academically, but I struggled with inappropriate behavior.

I started liking this girl in my class, Kelly. Kelly didn't necessarily like me back, but I was immature and messed with her anyway. What I didn't know was that Kelly had elder brothers who didn't have the greatest of reputations. First, her mom came to the school and told the administration about me picking on her, and I was called into the office. I was reprimanded by the principal to knock it off, or there would be major consequences, so I stopped. Then her brothers caught wind of their little sister being picked on and came up to the school looking for me. They ended up jumping on my friend, who they thought looked like me, and left him with a bloody nose. I found out the next day, and I instantly felt bad. I apologized to him, and most importantly, I apologized to Kelly for messing with her. That was the end of that crisis.

Every now and then, Luther would cut my brother's and my hair, and he typically would do a decent job. We had to sit still and not move our heads at all, or he would slap us. One day he thought it would be funny to give me what he called "a cool haircut." He cut all my hair off; I was completely bald and looked like a young Charles Barkley. I had to go to school and be completely ridiculed by friends and other kids. I got slapped in my head so many times that it started to turn red. Another time, he cut my hair and gave me a Mohawk. Mohawks are cool nowadays, but they were not cool back then, and once again, I was completely embarrassed.

I often peed in the bed and got whippings every time. One time I peed in the bed, and I had to go outside and pick my own switch off the tree. I know that the tendency would be to go pick the smallest branch off the tree, but unfortunately, that is not how that works. When you are told to get a switch, you are stuck with a tough dilemma: pick a switch that is big enough to satisfy the person who is going to whip you, or choose one that is not that big and won't hurt you as much. That is a lose-lose situation because both switches hurt, regardless of size, and that ended up being the case. I picked a switch that he didn't like, and he went to pick his own, which was much bigger, and he was extra mad because he had to go down there and pick out the branch after he told me to do it. Those whippings were bad, but nothing ever topped the extension cord whipping I received the year before.

Believe it or not, there were moments when Luther was a great dad. In his own particular way, he taught me ways to impress a girl and how to ride a bike for the first time. In fact, one of the fondest memories I have of him is when he took me and some of my siblings on a long bike ride across the city. That was the best time we ever spent together. Most of the time, I spent life despising him; but in that moment, he was loving and not harmful. He provided us with a memory that we could carry with us for the rest of our time living with him and my mother. It was that moment that made me realize why my mother had stayed with him for as long as she did.

I started to improve in Ms. Clarkson's class and didn't give her much trouble. I had done well in choir and started playing an instrument. I always excelled at PE because it was like getting a grade to have fun. Who doesn't love that? Ms. Clarkson was so cool. We had a special project where we had to turn "The Three Little Pigs" into a music video. We ended up using "Swing My Way" by KP and Envyi. Our adaptation of the song was "Piggy, Swing My Way." It sounded corny, but it was pretty cool and creative.

By the end of the school year, I had really navigated my way through third grade and was doing well. The last day of school, we had a dance. There happened to be a karaoke machine, and I had requested to sing "All My Life" by K-Ci and JoJo. I even had some of my friends sing backup. I could sing a little bit, and I caught the attention of everyone in the dance.

I even dedicated the song to Ms. Clarkson. Someone went to get her, and she was there while I serenaded her. I was quite the charmer for a third grader. When I finished, there was a big applause, and a lady came up to me at the end and said that I would be a star someday.

CHAPTER 7

Fire

The summer going into fourth grade was here, and it started off rocky. I got in trouble for something. It was probably minor, but nothing was minor in Luther's mind. Another whipping awaited me, but this time, another punishment was also waiting. He wanted me to stay in the corner for the entire summer. What that meant was that I would get up in the morning; go downstairs; eat breakfast, if there was any; and go into the corner. The only time I would be able to get out of the corner was if it was time to eat again or if I had to use the restroom. I was subjected to my own thoughts and staring at a blank white wall all day. If I turned around or wasn't standing straight, he would slap me on my head and force me to stand straight and face the wall. I had never been so happy to go to bed in my life, when it was time. I repeated this process for the next two days until my mother said enough was enough. Thank goodness, he listened to her that time. He felt I learned my lesson after three days.

I never liked *NASCAR* because I always associated that with him. He watched it every chance he got and even made us watch it with him. I grew to hate the sound of the cars going by the camera. I even despised the no. 3 car driven by Dale Earnhardt Sr., who was his favorite driver.

There was a sport that he did watch that I liked, and it was basketball. The finals were on, and it was Michael Jordan's Bulls versus the Utah Jazz. Jordan made some amazing plays in those finals, which Luther watched intently. I was too young to understand the greatness that was Michael Jordan.

A couple of weeks passed, and the day that I would never forget happened. This singular event was the beginning of major changes in my life. All my siblings were home, and we were being babysat by one of our neighbors from a different apartment building, whom we called our play cousin. My mom had found temporary work, and Luther was working his usual job. Our play cousin was helping me and my siblings get lunch without being prompted. We were downstairs making hot dogs and ramen—that seemed to be the go-to meal throughout my life.

The maintenance guys were in our apartment, working on something in the bathroom, so the apartment was full of people. My brother was upstairs, but we didn't know what he was doing. He was like a toddler; if he was quiet, he was probably doing something he had no business doing. My sister smelled smoke, so we immediately thought that it was the food, but we were boiling the food in water, so that wasn't the problem. We brushed it off and didn't think too much of it.

We called to Luther Jr. to come down, and he eventually did. Not ten minutes later, the maintenance guys came out of the bathroom, only to be met with smoke and flames. They yelled downstairs for everyone to get out of the apartment because there was a fire coming from my sisters' room. We all filed out of the apartment and made our way to the parking lot while we waited for the firefighter and for my mom and Luther to come from their jobs.

As we waited outside to figure out what the heck happened, we asked my brother what he did. He told us that he was in the closet playing trying to light incense sticks. My brother was always getting into something. I honestly thought that Luther would kill him when he got home because, in my mind, this was the worst thing that any of us could do.

In the moment of wondering what punishment was awaiting my brother, I realized that my brand-new shoes were up in flames. We didn't have very nice clothes or shoes, so whenever we did, we really cherished them. I cried when I thought about not getting those shoes back.

The firefighters arrived, and they started to put the fire out. Luther received a call about the apartment being on fire, and according to him, it saved his life because he was in a manhole that would've collapsed on him. I thought that it would've been nice if that happened. He would get a taste of his own medicine. My mom was the first to arrive; Luther arrived shortly after. My mom was in shock but relieved that we were okay. Luther tried to temper his anger and frustration.

The Red Cross provided us with a hotel for a couple of nights, as well as eating arrangements at a restaurant for a couple of days. We stayed at the Regency and ate out at the Point Restaurant, which served American-diner-type foods. Even though losing our home was a horrible circumstance, we were living the life for the moment because we rarely stayed in hotels, and we rarely ate out.

We got two rooms. My mom, Luther, and sisters were in one room; and my brother and I shared a room with our play cousin, who babysat us. The first night, I peed in the bed and was awakened by sounds of many voices in the room. My play cousin had brought some lady to the room, and they were having sex at the foot of the bed. I tried not to react, so I pretended that I was still asleep, which was hard with that going on.

After a couple of days, we had maxed out our Red Cross benefits of the free room and meals, so we moved to New Haven, a little town nearby, where my mom, Luther, and my four other siblings all stayed in one motel room. You can imagine how crowded and uncomfortable that was. We went from a three-bedroom apartment to one little motel room. We were not able to go back to our apartment because the landlord would not let us.

My question about whether my brother would be punished for this got answered: Luther threatened to beat my brother. He was so angry, but he couldn't do anything at the time because he would probably have ended up back in jail. He never did get that whipping. It was probably for the best.

While at the motel, we immediately looked for fun to partake in. There was a stream and park right behind our motel, where we played and had fun while Luther was at work. My mom would get frustrated waiting around at the motel until he got off work, so she got a job helping at the motel, cleaning rooms. I had to watch my siblings while she was out cleaning.

The first time she worked, she completed it so fast. When she got her pay for the day, she was surprised to find out that she got paid very little; I think she came back with $5. We ended up making the best of it by going to a restaurant across the street and getting a meal to share between the five of us. She realized that the longer she worked, the more she got paid, which meant I needed to take care of my siblings that much longer. It never really dawned on me that we were homeless. I just looked at it as being in a different situation from when we were in the apartment.

To give us some time away from the motel, my mother sent me to my grandfather Joe's house (Luther's dad) to stay with him for a couple of days, while my siblings stayed at an aunt's house. While there, I befriended some kids in the neighborhood who let me tag along with them to the local swimming pool, which was around the corner from my grandpa's house. I begged my grandpa to let me go swimming, and he did.

As I went with my new neighborhood friends, we went to the park, and none of them had money for us to get in. We had to sneak in by hopping the fence. We were very close to getting caught, but the people let us slide. They asked us if we hopped the fence, and we said no. They asked why we weren't wet, and we made up a story. It was clear that they didn't believe us, but luckily, they didn't feel like going through the trouble of kicking us out. We ended up having a lot of fun.

Those two days with Grandpa Joe were pretty cool. We ate at KFC and other fast-food places, and he had cable. At home, we rarely got the opportunity to watch what we wanted, so I was in heaven.

The time came for me to go back to the motel and back to reality—my reality, our reality. It would be a couple of more weeks at the motel before Luther was arrested for speeding. That meant that we couldn't stay in the motel anymore, and we needed a place to stay.

We went to stay with family friends back in Fort Wayne. They had a big house. There was a total of eleven people in the house, including us.

They really welcomed us into their home, and we were so grateful. I made my first scrambled eggs in that house, but they were really salty. They still said, "Good try."

My mom got a job exotic dancing. While she was at work, we were babysat by the daughters of the home. They were so good to us. I know we weren't on our best behavior at times, but they would let us go outside, and they played with us. They even taught me how to play basketball by cutting out the bottom of a milk crate and nailing it to a tree. We also walked to Phil's Market, which was a five-minute walk from the house, to get snacks and goodies.

A couple of weeks had passed, and my mom found a place for us to stay, with the help of her cousin. We were getting ready to move again.

CHAPTER 8

Abbey

Our new house was a two-bedroom in a decent neighborhood, also in Fort Wayne. We were a block away from the very huge McMillen Park. We played there often. Luther was still in jail, and we weren't sure when he was getting out. Mom was still exotic dancing at night, but life was starting to gain some normalcy.

School was set to start soon for me, Mercedes, and Junior. We attended Bailey Elementary, where I seemed to do well. By this time, I was in fourth grade. My grades were good, and I mostly stayed out of trouble. The only thing that was not so great about the school was that I got picked on by a kid in our class. His name was Leon. He was set on making life tough for me. Whenever we went to recess, he picked the teams and put everyone that was good on his team; the rest of us had to be on the other teams. He pushed me at times and was always making fun of my clothes. As I mentioned, I had an issue with peeing in the bed, and there were times when I came to school smelling like pee because we didn't have a washer and dryer to have fresh clothes.

I was an open target, but I did befriend one person. His name was Garrett, and we lived a couple of blocks from each other. We got to know each other well enough that I stayed at his house and played video games. Being at his house was like being at my old best friend Christian's house. It allowed me to get away from the struggles in my life, and I saw what it was like to not have to worry about where the next meal was coming from. I would usually go to his house to hang out and sometimes spend the night, but he only came over to my house once, which I would regret.

I didn't want to invite people to the house because we didn't have much, but I felt like we were good enough friends that it wouldn't matter. When he came over, everything was fine until my mom wanted me to boil some water because we didn't have hot water at the time. We would use the water to wash dishes, take a bath, or anything else you could think of that required hot water. I didn't think anything of it until we were at school the next day, and he was making fun of me that I had to boil water. Most of the kids at recess began to call me poor. I tried to turn the tables on him because he had rats in his house that left poop in his underwear drawer, but the damage had already been done.

When I got home, I felt sad and thought that school wasn't going to get better. That night, while eating dinner, I broke down crying because I just couldn't take the hurt, and Mom couldn't do anything about it. She tried her best.

Within a week, Mom brought home a black Labrador retriever. This dog had been trained well, and she loved so hard. We loved her back. We took her on walks and to the park to play fetch. Her name was Abbey, and boy, we loved that dog.

One day when we were going to school, my mom was not home yet because of another long night at the strip club. I asked my sister Mercedes to put the dog on the leash so we could go to school, which was probably a bad idea. Abbey had lost her collar, and my sister tied the leash around the dog's neck. When we got home from school, a chunk of Abbey's neck was on one side of the leash, and her eyes were bloodshot. I was so mad at my sister. I couldn't do anything but get frustrated and hope that Abbey would be okay. She was fine, but man, was that scary! Abbey became family to us.

Then it happened. Whenever Abbey had to use the restroom, we would let her out in the backyard, but we didn't have a fence. She usually would stay in the yard to do her business and then scratch on the door to come back inside.

One night Mom let Abbey out the front door in the middle of the night because she had to use the restroom, and after about five minutes, Mom heard a loud bang. She looked outside, and she saw that Abbey had been hit by a car. She brought Abbey into the house and laid her on the floor. My mom began to play Master P.'s "I Miss My Homies," and I was wondering what the heck was going on. I got out of bed and went into the living room, only to be met with Abbey's lifeless body. I immediately questioned my mother about what happened and why Abbey was bleeding and not moving. She just shook her head, said that Abbey was hit by a car, and apologized.

I was so heartbroken. I couldn't understand why this was happening to our family or why every time we had something good, it was taken away from us. The one thing that I could look forward to after school, the one being that loved me just as much as I loved it, was gone. It was so tough to experience that.

The next day, I was on the school bus, and I burst out crying. When asked what was wrong, I told them that my dog had died, and people didn't think that was a good reason to cry. In fact, the bus driver said, "Boy, I thought it was something more serious." She just didn't understand. That dog was everything and more, and she provided so much comfort to our home. It was devastating.

We attempted to replace Abbey right away with a puppy that was a German shepherd–Rottweiler mix. We didn't have any experience training a dog because Abbey came to us trained already. The dog ended up peeing and crapping everywhere. That was so annoying.

Our neighbors across the street had a huge Great Dane. They usually kept it locked up because they didn't want it terrorizing the neighborhood. It finally got out one day, and unfortunately, my brother was its victim. He was playing outside, and the Great Dane bit my brother in the face. He had to get stitches, and he still has the mark on his face. It was safe to say I was done with animals because I concluded that no dog would ever be like Abbey, and we shouldn't try to replace her. I haven't had a pet since then.

CHAPTER 9

I Just Want to Skate

My tenth birthday was not filled with fanfare. Mom did the best she could; she really did, but times were hard, and I completely understood. That day was the first time I tried fish at one of the local fish markets, and it was love at first taste. I even got a chance to stay the night at the house of another friend who lived a couple of houses down. We ended up playing Nintendo 64 until our fingers were numb and our eyelids were heavy. That was a cool day, and it was another opportunity to forget the struggles of our lives.

I remember nights when we didn't have much to eat, and one night my uncle Bo came by, went into our pantry, and grabbed random ingredients just so he could put together a meal that would feed our big family. He ended up doing a good job, considering we didn't have much. We were grateful for the gesture, but we didn't appreciate the bland food he made.

A couple of more weeks passed, and I was beginning to know more kids in the neighborhood. I must've rubbed some people the wrong way because a group of guys, who happened to be brothers, felt it necessary to jump on me. I went home and told my cousin Sierra, who babysat us at times. She was not happy, and she proclaimed that we were going to find them and fight them. It didn't take us long before we found them, and they were still laughing about jumping on me earlier. She told them if they jumped in while I was fighting them one by one, then she would jump in. They agreed, and I ended up beating them up one by one. I thought I was the coolest thing since sliced bread. We laughed about it, but as I look back, I still can't believe that worked.

Because we were so strapped for cash, I went to the local convenience store to see if the manager needed help with anything. I was only ten years old, but I wanted to do anything I could to help my family. The manager usually needed help, so I helped him with things around the store, and I was paid in things we needed for the home, like dish soap. That seemed to help the family out very much.

It became super-apparent that we didn't have much money when our class was slated to go roller-skating at the local roller dome, and we needed just $5 to go on the field trip. I approached Mom, begged her to let me go, and asked if she had the money, but she just couldn't come up with it. I had to go to school the next day and inform my teacher that I could not come up with the money, and I was told that I couldn't go on the field trip. I was devastated, and to make matters worse, my old nemesis—Leon—laughed and made fun of me for being poor and not able to furnish the $5 for the field trip. My class went on the trip without me, and I was forced to stay in in-school suspension (ISS). It was not my first time in ISS, but this was the first time I had to be in there for something I had absolutely no control over.

I ended up getting redemption a month or so later; the school rented roller skates, and we were able to skate for free in the gym. That required a permission slip, which my mom gladly signed for me. I brought it back so I could skate, and guess who didn't bring his and wasn't able to skate? That's right—Leon. He tried to make fun of me and pointed out the fact that I couldn't skate when it cost me but that I was all over it when it was free, but he couldn't bring me down that day. I would have my opportunities to defend myself and make fun of him for being fat, but I can't lie and say he didn't affect me.

Mom was still working at the strip club, and things started to go downhill from there. The first night that my mom brought home guys from the strip club, I knew that it was exposing us to something that none of us were ready for. I think she tried to justify it by saying we needed the extra cash, but it was tough to have to shield my siblings from that. Then the inevitable happened: I found a used crack pipe in my mom's room. I didn't ever see her using it, but I had an idea that she did.

Mom had a reliable mode of transportation in the car that Luther got before he was arrested. She didn't have the money to make payments, and collections would come and try to get the car. Mom did her best to evade them, but they finally got the car, and we were carless at that point. We had a rough winter that year because we had been hit with a blizzard. There were about two feet of snow in our front yard, and school was canceled. It turned out to be a cold winter.

It was only a matter of time before something had to give. The New Year was on us, and my mom informed me, being the eldest, that my siblings and I would be moving in with my grandmother, who was Luther's stepmother, and that we wouldn't be living with her anymore. I said okay and awaited the next adventure. We had been through so much, the biggest thing being the apartment fire the previous summer, that I was numb to any new surprises that were awaiting me.

As we rode over to Grandma's, I thought about what was next. I wondered what would become of our new home and neighborhood and if they would be happy places to stay. There were so many questions, but one thing was for sure: we weren't going to be living with Luther.

CHAPTER 10

Granny

We had been to Grandma's house before. Luther took us there to hang out with family numerous times. In fact, Grandma had these creepy dolls that sat in one of the windowsills that was high on the wall, and it scared the crap out of me. That's what I remember most about her home. I knew the neighborhood was quiet. I also knew that life was going to be a little different from what we knew it to be.

As we arrived, Grandma welcomed us with open arms, and the thing that was so apparent was her calming spirit. That spirit has stayed with her until this day. At that time, Grandma was living in a big house that she had lived in for years. It had a huge basement, five bedrooms, two bathrooms, and plenty of backyard space that would be host to my imagination.

Grandma had recently divorced Luther's father, who happened to be the grandfather I stayed with after the apartment fire. My two aunts were the only ones living with my grandmother before we arrived. Grandma was a home health aide, working the second shift. My aunts were a tad annoyed with our arrival, which was understandable. It was a quiet home that would turn into a rambunctious one in a matter of a day.

My mom let us know that this would be temporary, just until she got back on her feet. She promised that she would visit often and keep in touch. Little did we know that we would never get a chance to live with my mother again. She ended up going to jail within a month of dropping us off.

My mom drove off, and we were shown our sleeping quarters. My brother and I would get my uncle's old room, and my sisters would share a room with my grandma. It was now a house of five kids (ten, eight, seven, six, and two years old) and three adults. Fortunately (unfortunately for me), we would still be able to go to Bailey Elementary as there was a bus stop close to the house.

The routine at Granny's went something like this: we attended school, and afterward, Grandma would make us go to the Weston Park Youth Center, a.k.a. the Center, once our homework was done. This was the place that literally changed the course of my life.

Our first time at the Center was overwhelming. I didn't know what to expect. In fact, I was nervous, but the staff welcomed us with open arms. The Center was in the middle of a park, so it had basketball and tennis courts, baseball fields, and jungle gyms. Inside the Center, they had pool tables, Ping-Pong tables, foosball, and several rooms with different activities, including a computer room. They also had a kitchen and an auditorium with a stage. It was a kid's dream. Just about every kid in the neighborhood went to the Center after school and stayed until it closed or it was time for them to go home. It became a place where we were safe and free to be whoever we wanted to be.

When we left the Center to go home, a meal was usually waiting on us, cooked by my granny if she wasn't at work or by my eldest aunt, Sherrie. It was refreshing to have that much fun, get a warm meal, take a warm bath or shower, and sleep in a comfortable bed.

Granny did her best to make sure we were comfortable, but she also wasn't a pushover. She whipped us when we needed it, not because it was the thing to do. I don't know if a kid ever needs a whipping, but when slave mentality is inherited and becomes a way of life, this becomes the norm. This punishment was not anything like Luther's. Grandma had to establish that she meant business. Living there was better than we were used to, but we needed to do our part. The first time I got a whipping by Granny, it hurt more than I expected. I had talked back to my teacher, and she let me know that wasn't tolerated.

At school, things were better in the sense that we were not struggling for cash or having to watch Mom do whatever it took to put food on the table. Granny made sure that we went to school with clean clothes. They weren't name brands, which my bully and classmates made sure to remind me of by making fun of me. We were frequent shoppers at Payless, and boy, did I get teased when I went to school. Granny did the best with what she had, and we sure gave her some extra gray hairs.

Grandma let it be known that we were to get up every Sunday and go to church. We woke up to *Bobby Jones Gospel* on the television and the sweet aroma of White Diamonds, my granny's favorite perfume. It smelled good to me, and that was how we knew it was time for our Sunday best. We were dressed and ready to go by 9:40 a.m. Church started at ten and was a five-minute drive. Grandma had her special row in the church, and we sat with her, listening intently.

My favorite part of church was the choir. I loved whenever the choirs got up to sing. The band would play with such grace and ease, and the different choirs would grace us with their beautiful voices. We had a general choir, men's choir, women's choir, and more.

Every Sunday lent itself to an adventure. Whenever the pastor would preach, it was hard to pay attention, and I would fall asleep, like most kids who can't sit still. Grandma would not allow that. I mainly would get pinched in the back of my arm if I fell asleep, so I tried to stay awake. Sometimes it was just too tough.

After church, we normally went home; but every couple of Sundays, we went with my grandmother to drop off her time sheets from work all the way to the north side of Fort Wayne. We often tried to get her to let us have McDonald's, but she hit us with the line that I'm sure every kid has heard: "Do you have McDonald's money?" Whenever we heard that, we knew that we weren't going to get McDonald's. We also would pass by Golden Corral, but we could not persuade her to let us eat there either. We would eat at both places on special occasions but not every weekend.

It's interesting how we went from barely eating meals to eating meals consistently to being picky. Granny would spoil us with one of her many delicious home-cooked meals. She was born in Mississippi, so she had a knack for cooking up some good soul food. My favorite meal that she made was spaghetti and fried catfish. It was so delicious. I looked forward to eating that every time. I didn't even know that catfish went with spaghetti until she made it. Anytime my granny made beans, whether it was black-eyed peas or great northern beans, you could count on those to be accompanied by her amazing corn bread, which was so delicious.

We were eating well when we lived with Granny. If there was something that we didn't want to eat, my granny didn't make us eat it. The first time she told me that I didn't have to eat something, I was so surprised because we didn't have that luxury when we lived with my mom and Luther. She told me that if we didn't want something, we didn't have to eat it, but we better not waste it.

I instantly got on my granny's bad side because of my bed-wetting issues. She couldn't understand why I peed in the bed so much, and I couldn't understand it either. I would not drink anything before bed. I would use the restroom before bed and still pee in it. Granny would get mad because I would pee and then hide it because I didn't want to get in trouble. Every time I returned from school, Granny was waiting on me to explain myself.

We had tried medicine, diapers, anything to try to alleviate this issue. At ten years old, I didn't want to be caught wearing diapers, but we had to try anything we could. We even had to warn people about it if I stayed the night somewhere. It was so embarrassing. Granny and I tried to figure something out to help me stop peeing in the bed, but nothing worked, and I was miserable. I would punch myself, out of frustration, for peeing in the bed. I asked myself why I couldn't get up to pee. It was tough to deal with, and it was the thing I struggled with the most when I lived with Granny. I eventually stopped peeing in the bed when I got older.

School was smoother as time went on. My grades stayed steady, despite all that was going on. Granny made sure to encourage me to stay on top of my studies. She was always giving me accolades every time I brought home a good grade. When I didn't do well, she supported me and helped me get back on track. In my fourth-grade class, I studied so hard for the spelling bee so I could compete against classmates, and she was there for me. I was so prepared that I ended up being in the top two in my class, which qualified me to compete against all the other qualifiers in the school.

As we were on the stage, getting through the competition, my first word came up, and I nailed it. More students started to drop out, and it was my turn again. The word was *dolphin*. "Dolphin, D-O-L-F-I-N, dolfin?"

Buzz! I knew how to spell it. I practiced the word. The pressure of the moment got to me, and that word haunted me. When I told Granny, she told me that I would get them next time and that I was the twentieth out of all the kids in the school. She was so supportive.

Fourth grade was also the time when I started to discover music. I learned how to play the recorder. We also got a chance to sing in choir class. My bully was getting less and less ammo to use against me, and that was refreshing.

At home, things were going well, with the exception of the usual arguments with my siblings. I fought with my little brother often. He couldn't seem to leave my things alone. We also didn't like the same things. He was always into Hot Wheels, firefighters, and police. I was always into sports, and I tried to get him to play with me, but he never got into it. We even differed when it came to video games. We played those together, but I liked sports.

Since he didn't like sports, I played in our backyard by myself a lot. I made my own basketball team, soccer team, or whatever sport I could play in the backyard. My basketball team consisted of me, me, and me. I was every position, and I won a championship every season. I would pass the ball to myself and everything. It was elaborate. When I wasn't playing outside by myself, I was going to the Center, even during the summer. They had a summer program once school was out.

I finished fourth grade on a high note, and I was ready to take on fifth. At the Center, I was really starting to come into my own. I gained a few friends. One was named Stephan. We were the same age and went to the same school but had different classes. We both had a few sisters. He was the eldest as well. Every time I went to the Center, I made sure to see if he was there. We would play any of the games in the Center, but we mainly played in the computer room, where they had a Nintendo 64 and *Super Mario Kart*. That game was endless fun. We also were superfans of *Pokémon* and would talk about the show and even trade *Pokémon* cards together. He was my first best friend from the Center, and I really relied on him for company whenever we went there.

We also joined a singing and dancing group with Ms. Sandra, who would come to the Center once a week and teach us how to dance and sing. We got made fun of for being the only boys in the group, but we both stuck through it until we were older and couldn't take the class anymore. We enjoyed it while we were in it. We performed a couple of times. One time we performed in front of hundreds of people, and it was great. We also sang the popular gospel songs "Joyful, Joyful" and "Oh Happy Day" enough times for both of those songs to be ingrained in my memory forever. I was the only one who could hit the high note by the lead singer in "Oh Happy Day"; I was flexing my vocal muscles. We even participated in a fashion show.

The Center provided many opportunities for us to blossom and really understand our potential. The moment that really affected my life was when I joined Stop the Madness, a mentoring program put together by Mr. Ben Hayes. He, along with other black male contributing members of the city, would come to the Center every Tuesday. He brought in pizza so he could entice us to come and have a conversation, and it worked.

The conversation centered on the book *Talks My Father Never Had with Me*. The book had many different topics of discussion that sparked great conversation even for a ten-year-old. We learned how to shake a man's hand and why we shouldn't wear our pants sagging. Mr. Hayes did not play that. He wouldn't allow it. He made sure that we didn't enter into his space with our pants saggin' as it should be. Mr. Hayes gave us opportunities to be young men and have positive male role models to look up to.

Tuesday was when we got to learn vital information, and every now and then, we went on a field trip. Being as poor as we were before we lived with Granny, we didn't go to many places. We took family trips, maybe one time to Indianapolis, but that was it. When we got a chance to see new things, it was eye-opening and awe-inspiring. The first trip that we took was to an Indiana Pacers game. The Pacers are a team in the NBA. We got to travel on a coach bus to get to Indianapolis from our hometown of Fort Wayne, and we arrived at Conseco Fieldhouse, home of the Pacers. It was my first time attending a professional sport event, and it wouldn't be the last.

We took many more trips, including more Pacers games, a trip to Chicago to a museum, and a trip to Cedar Point, an amusement park in Sandusky, Ohio. That trip was one of the best days of my life. I had never been on roller coasters, and I was like a kid in a candy store. The first ride I got on was the Blue Streak, which was a wooden roller coaster. I was so scared that I was holding on to a stranger. He didn't like that, but I didn't care. I also got on other rides that scared the crap out of me, but nothing or no one could take that high from me. On the way home from Cedar Point, my voice had essentially gone out, and I tried to participate in a singing contest. The people on the bus were so impressed with how I sang. Those trips really allowed me to see more than my small hometown.

My siblings were too young to fully experience everything that I did. My brother would often get into trouble at the Center. One time the Center was holding a candy fund-raiser, and my brother had stolen money from the sales. I probed him on how he got the money, and he said he got it from a family member. In my excitement, completely not investigating this further, I got some money from him and went to the local mom-and-pop convenience store, Brownlee's.

When I arrived back at the Center, all hell had broken loose. I was pulled in to talk with one of the workers, who investigated me like I was a criminal. It turned out my brother had stolen the money. They had him in there and my cousin Daniel, whom they had to chase down and find because my brother gave him money as well. My cousin lived with his mother, a block away from the Center.

I was so frustrated with my brother because he did stuff like this often. He stole my stuff, and I would get so mad with him. We fought and argued often because we were so different. I was so angry with him this time because he lied, and part of it was my fault because I should've known, but I pretended like that was rational that he would get money from family like that.

When Granny found out, we knew we were in deep trouble. We had been suspended from the Center. My brother was suspended for a week, and I was only suspended for a couple of days. I was mad at him for that and for the whipping we ended up getting after Granny found out. We were going to be stuck in the house. No attending the Center for us.

Shortly after the suspension, I continued to attend the Center after I apologized for taking part in the thievery. The Center also offered Saturday school, which I dreaded going to but went anyway. I couldn't believe that Granny would make me and my siblings go to school on a Saturday, but I'm ultimately glad we did. The Center director was very much into black history and African culture. We learned about Ghanaian language and culture as well as our own history. The people who attended the Center were predominantly black, so that was why he made it a point to really teach us our culture and history. Every Saturday, we would attend the school at the Center for a couple of hours and learn our history. It was intriguing, and I wouldn't fully understand it until I was older.

As the school year drew near, the Center would take a trip to Toronto, Canada, to attend the Afro-Caribbean Festival. Since Mercedes and I were the eldest of my other siblings and attended every Saturday, we qualified to go on this trip. It was the first time that either of us traveled out of the country, and it was another opportunity to partake in a completely new adventure.

Once we told Granny, there was no hesitation. She gave us permission to go and paid all the fees that were required. I was so excited as I was for many of the trips that we took. I had everything packed and ready to go, and Granny would always pack up some new toiletries, socks, and underwear. We were always fresh. We left that evening, and Mr. Sanders, one of the chaperones, picked us up in his van, and we were on our way.

We all met at the Center and headed up north. The drive was a little over six hours. To some, it seemed like forever; to me, it was an adventure that I didn't want to end. When we arrived at the border, the Canadian Border Patrol spoke to the driver, and we were on our way. I was so amazed by the speed-limit signs that read "105," not quite understanding that it was kilometers and not miles per hour.

When we arrived, we checked into our hotel, and then we went to the mall. I exchanged some of my dollars for Canadian money, and I thought that I was rich because I got more Canadian money for my dollar. We also ate at a fish-and-chips place, and that was when I learned that they called French fries chips. They also had a McDonald's that had a Double Big Mac on the menu, which was hard to believe, but they had it.

We also visited Wonderland, which was an amusement park. That turned out to be a fun day as well. I rode some awesome rides and really enjoyed myself. I was having so much fun on the trip. We also went swimming in the hotel pool every day we were there, and my sister and I ended up paying the price of swimming so much.

We ended the trip by going to Caribana, an Afro-Caribbean festival, which was so awe-inspiring. It was great to experience so much of the different cultures and food. I danced and enjoyed every bit of it. As the last night ended, I started to get upset because I didn't want this fun to end, but we were due to head home.

When we got back, my sister and I complained about earaches, so my granny brought us to the doctor. We came down with swimmer's ear, which was some form of ear infection caused by constant swimming. The doctor prescribed medicine, and it cleared up within a few days. Other than that blemish, we really enjoyed ourselves on the trip to Canada and looked forward to our next adventure.

CHAPTER 11

Talent

The new school year was on us, and I was now in fifth grade. I had two different teachers because our full-time teacher was unable to teach a full day, so they brought in another one for the afternoon. I thought it was cool, and they thought it would better prepare us for sixth grade, when we were to have multiple teachers.

The school year would be just as smooth as it ended. Granny had instilled a sense of stability. The things that were distracting us from school were down to a minimum. In fact, the only two things that were bothersome were having to meet with a caseworker and visiting my mom while she was in jail. We had to meet with the caseworker because we were in foster care, even though I saw it as just staying with Granny.

Whenever our caseworker visited our school, I instantly got embarrassed. It was so difficult to keep nosy kids out of our business, and I didn't want anyone to know what that was about. I also had a hard time visiting my mom while she was incarcerated. It was tough to see her in a place where she couldn't be with us or have any freedom to do as she pleased. Some would say she deserved it; I say, with her upbringing, she never got a fair chance. She wasn't the same mother I knew while she was in jail, and after I saw what those drugs did to her health, I started to feel ashamed that she was my mom. I never told anyone in school that my mother was in jail. The last thing I needed was to provide more ammo to my bully.

The two-teacher classroom was cool. It kept us on our toes with excitement. The teachers had different styles, but it was such a seamless transition. I continued to get good grades, but I still had issues with my behavior. My nemesis, Leon, was still terrorizing me on the playground, but things at home were better.

Things really started to turn around when it was announced that there would be a talent show. I immediately went to my friend Stephan to see if he would be interested. He was apprehensive, but he was down to do it. We both went to Ms. Sandra to solicit help with our dance, and we both agreed to dance to the popular song at that time "I Like It" by Sammie. I knew that song would be poppin', and if we nailed the dance, we could really make our mark. She worked with us until we were ready, and boy, were we ready.

I wasn't as nervous as my friend. The event started off well with a couple of acts. When it was our turn and the music began to play, the crowd went crazy. We started to dance, and the crowd went into a frenzy. We performed flawlessly, and I even threw in some extra gyrations for the ladies. My friend thought I was doing too much there but whatever. When we finished, the whole gym was lit up with excitement, and we dared anyone else to top that performance. One of the black male teachers gave us mad props and told us we were too grown for our age.

One of the acts to follow us was my nemesis, Leon, and his friends doing what looked like dancing to the same song we chose. Everyone agreed that we did the song the most justice, and that was awesome. When we went home that day on the bus, I got into a confrontation with a kid from another class and ended up being punched in the face. I didn't cry, but I was visibly shaken up, and Leon consoled me. He never really picked on me after that. I believe I earned his respect when I impressed him during our dance performance. He no longer saw me as a short pip-squeak.

October that year was the first time I went to the Circle City Classic. It was held in Indianapolis. The Classic, as it was aptly named, was a football game between two historically black colleges. The game was mediocre, but the activities surrounding the game were the bigger deal, including the Battle of the Bands. Nothing got me more hyped than watching the bands battle and play songs that we were familiar with. We went to two different Classic games after that, and the bands delivered every time. It really helped me see black folks in a positive light.

The first Christmas at Granny's house was awesome. Granny, with the help of our caseworker—whom we began seeing shortly after moving in with Granny—got connected with a church to give us a lot of presents. Our caseworker would only visit every now and then and ask us how things were at home and school. I was now eleven years old, so I was okay with anyone who was nice; my siblings felt the same. It was a stark contrast to the Christmas we had the year prior. I got a lot of presents, including two basketballs.

That year, my uncle Gary came home for the holidays from Indiana University (IU) Bloomington, so I got to play his Dreamcast, which was something else that was supercool about living at Granny's. We mainly tried to stay out of the way of my youngest aunt, Maya, but we did get along when it came to wrestling. She loved wrestling, and we watched it with her. I started to really admire the Rock, Stone Cold Steve Austin, and all those old-school wrestling guys. *Monday Night Raw* was awesome, especially after a big pay-per-view and *Sunday Night Heat* would cap off my weekend. We never ordered a pay-per-view, so we had to watch the next day to see what happened. That was what we had in common.

During the Dr. Martin Luther King Jr. holiday, my mentor Mr. Hayes put on a youth empowerment seminar to inspire and motivate the youth. It was held at Southland High School, and it was cool because we didn't have to be in school. I was still doing well with my grades, so Mr. Hayes made sure to include me in as many things as possible. The speaker for the seminar was Bill Cartwright, who played with the Chicago Bulls and was Michael Jordan's teammate. We all thought that was pretty cool, and we learned a lot that day.

The one moment that stuck with me was my interaction that day with the mayor of Fort Wayne. He was scheduled to be there, and I had never met him before. He had just been elected, and he just so happened to show up to the event. Mr. Hayes has always given me the credit for what happened next, but he empowered me to speak with confidence. I saw him doing important things for the community, and I wanted to be the same way. I met the mayor, gave him a firm handshake, and told him that together we could do great things. He was so impressed as was my mentor. In fact, the mayor mentioned me in his State of the City address as a defining moment of his time as mayor. Mr. Hayes never let me forget that moment. He reminds me every time we talk to each other.

CHAPTER 12

Unwanted Change

The caseworker continued to visit us at home. I didn't realize what it meant; I just thought that I was living with Granny. I wasn't aware that I was part of the system. The caseworker meetings were pretty routine. She came, asked how we were doing, and then continued to ask questions about everything that was currently going on. As my life continued to get more stable, seeing the caseworker was the one thing that reminded me that we weren't in a normal situation. It wasn't "home sweet home" whenever she visited, and she was about to turn our world upside down.

I had finished fifth grade and was hopeful that sixth grade would bring more good cheer. We ended fifth grade with a bang by going to the skating rink (how ironic). There wasn't a disappointment this time, just good vibes. It was also bittersweet because when I went to Bailey, it was far from where we were living, but Granny let me finish out the year with friends. Most of my classmates, if not all, were slated to go to one of two middle schools, Laney or Grayhawk, both in better neighborhoods. I was one of the few slated to go to a middle school outside of those two. I was going to Kingston Middle School. We spent that last day saying goodbye to one another, and I prepared to move on to a school in my area.

As the summer began, Granny had to pick Uncle Gary up from college. He was graduating, so we planned to watch him graduate and then bring him back home to Fort Wayne. The drive to Bloomington was about three hours. This seemed like a lot when I was younger, but it wasn't too bad.

Granny rented a new Ford Explorer, and my other uncle Nate came with us so he could help her drive. That would be my first of a few trips to IU. It was another experience that helped me see college as a tangible thing, not something that was out of reach.

As we drove down to Bloomington, I always admired the cornfields, rolling hills, and open road. It was a two-lane highway, and if you weren't driving fast enough, then you needed to get out of the way. I love my granny, but she wasn't the fastest driver. It was a good thing that Uncle Nate did the bulk of the driving because we were going to get there faster.

As we arrived on campus, I was enamored with its pure beauty. The city was pristine, but you could tell it was built as a college town. The buildings were old but elegant, and there was history all over the place. It was a huge campus, spread acres and acres apart. We arrived in time to see the ceremony, which was held at the football stadium. It was huge, but unfortunately, the team wasn't any good. If you know anything about Indiana, then you know that Indiana is a basketball state. Although the football team wasn't any good, the basketball team at IU was great.

There were so many people in the stadium for the graduation. It was another great moment when I got to experience something of that magnitude. This experience gave me an opportunity to see myself on a college campus, and it was almost a given that I was going to college. It was so cool to see my uncle Gary walk across the stage in that huge stadium. After the ceremony, we met with him at his dorm, and we helped pack his stuff into the SUV. His dorm was pretty cool. We got something to eat, and we were on our way back to Fort Wayne.

As the summer continued, Granny eventually got tired of me being in the house when I wasn't going to the Center. She recommended (more like demanded) that I go to summer school. Think about the magnitude of that: she wanted me to go to a school that I was going to for the first time and essentially not know anyone because I was coming from a different school in the other part of town. I was so nervous, and I begged and pleaded with my granny to not make me go, but I had to. It turned out to not be so bad, and I ended up making friends, going into the school year.

That same summer, I went to my first Indiana Black Expo. The Black Expo was an event where all people, mostly black, congregated in Indianapolis to experience a wealth of information, good food, and amazing entertainment. There were events for the teens and for the adults. I attended the youth leadership seminar, where we did workshops during the day and fun activities at night, including a celebrity basketball game. David Banner performed at the halftime show that year. I was in awe because he was so close. We also went to a B2K concert that year, and I was upset because we had to go. The girls were excited, though. It ended up being a fun time, but I wasn't going to admit that. And of course, there was swimming. We swam a lot at the hotel.

Another fun-filled summer had me put the life of strife and hardship behind me, and I pondered about what my future might entail. The possibilities were endless, and this was the first time I started to envision a bright future for myself.

Oh, life does have a funny way of slapping you in the face. Remember when I said my caseworker was going to flip our world upside down? Luther was out of jail, and he was beginning the process of getting us back from Granny. If there was one thing that he was good at, it was maneuvering the court system. The man worked his way around a courtroom like a figure skater in the Winter Olympics. He was graceful and knew what to do and what to say.

Granny broke the news to me. I was devastated. I counted down the days until they made it official. I told her that I didn't want to go because of how he treated us in the past, but she couldn't do anything. I just could not understand how a court could allow a man who was so abusive and so mean-spirited to be able to take in five kids. Who are they trying to protect when they keep the kids with unfit biological parents? It was frustrating, and I tried my best to argue against it, to no avail. We were going to live with Luther again.

Weeks turned to days; hours turned to minutes. The day came for him to come pick us up. I went upstairs to see if there were any last-minute things I needed to get, but I had everything. As I looked around the room, I began to cry uncontrollably because I didn't want to go. Just when we were starting to gain some stability, they thought it would be wise for us to not only have to go to another school but also live with the man who caused my family so much hurt and pain. I gathered myself and wiped my tears because I didn't want him to know how sad I was, and I went downstairs to say goodbye to Granny. We walked out of the house to Luther's van, and I waved goodbye to Granny.

CHAPTER 13

Return of Luther

I continued to try to hide the fact that I was not happy with this move, and Luther told me to cheer up. I took those words with a grain of salt. There wasn't much he could tell me that would assure me of my safety or that life would be as good as it had been with Granny. As we arrived at our new home, north of Granny's house, we were introduced to Luther's girlfriend or friend; I didn't know what or who she was to him. We would later get clarification. In the home lived this lady and her two daughters. With the five of us and Luther, it was a full house.

I wanted so much for the past to not repeat itself, and it turned out that it didn't. Luther seemed to be a different person, more caring and less angry. I still can't figure out what changed. Maybe the thought of having kids in the system scared him. But he had left kids before to be orphans. Maybe he missed being with us. He had a rough way of showing his affection for us in the past. Maybe he was less stressed because he wasn't with my mom anymore, and she was in jail. All I knew was that he was different.

One day my siblings and I were outside playing. There was an abandoned house, one house down from ours. We played on the handicap ramp because we could get good speed with our play car down the ramp. I got angry about something that was going on, and I picked up the car and threw it. I ended up breaking the window. I knew I would be in so much trouble, so I gathered all my siblings and went in the house.

When Luther found out I broke the window, he didn't do anything. That would've resulted in a grade A butt whipping while at Willowbrook, so I knew things were different. He didn't keep us locked up in the house; we were free to go outside or to the local park. Things were turning out for the best. I was beginning to think that maybe this wasn't so bad.

A different home in a different neighborhood meant that I wasn't in Kingston's borders. That meant I was going to a different school, Lakeland Middle. All that preparation and making new friends in summer school was for naught. I didn't know many people, and I was going into a completely new situation.

A couple of weeks into the school year, we did a mock vote for the president of the United States. I voted for Al Gore because I was told to vote Democrat, and for whatever reason, I thought people agreed with me. When they announced that Bush won the school vote and it wasn't close, I realized that not everyone thought like me. In fact, I had disagreed with a good chunk of the school. That was a lot to take in for a sixth grader.

During this time, I began to develop this idea that I was superior to my white classmates. For some reason, one I can't explain, I believed that I should not lose a fight to a white student. I established the idea that I, a black boy, should easily beat up a white boy. How I came up with this logic, I couldn't tell you. It is possible I established this while learning about black history at the Center. The anger and frustration of reading about my ancestors being bullied for so long must have given me this idea. Maybe it allowed me to avenge their pain. At any rate, I wanted to put this theory to the test by checking this white kid who happened to be talking smack.

To my surprise, he decided not to back down. I challenged him to a fight and told him to meet me in the restroom. The word about the fight got around, and as we went to the restroom, there was a slight crowd of different people gathering, including boys who were in higher grades than us. As the kid stared me down, I laughed because I was confident I could beat him up. I decided that I wasn't going to fight him but instead give him a swirly. I grabbed his head, overpowering him, and put his head in the toilet for a good ole swirly.

Another student warned us that a teacher was coming, so I let him go and pretended like nothing was going on. I got lucky that day that the teacher didn't have evidence I did anything to him. He definitely suspected that something was going on. I'm not sure what happened to that kid after that. I'm glad that situation didn't get worse. It seemed those years of being bullied so much turned into me being the bully, and this was a habit I needed to kick.

Things at school continued to mellow out. My mentor established a mentoring group that met once a week during our lunchtime. I was excited that I still got a chance to see him. I also joined the cross-country team. When I told Luther, he laughed, but he was happy I was participating in a sport.

The real reason I ran was because there was a girl on the team who liked me. She was white with short hair. She was a cute girl, but I couldn't get over the fact that she had short hair. I was a jerk, I know. I barely got over the fact that she was white because, at the time, I didn't feel comfortable dating outside my race. Even though I had witnessed interracial dating with Luther post-Mom, every girlfriend I had up until then was black. We would sneak off and do our own thing during long runs, until I finally called it quits with her and cross-country. I was intent on waiting for track season, where I was most comfortable.

Luther continued to be a different man. He was good to us, but he didn't change the way he treated women. He wasn't beating on them, not that I remember, but he also wasn't faithful. We were in the middle of one of his love triangles. At that time, we had Laurie, whom we moved in with, but I don't know if Luther liked her as more than a friend. I honestly think he was using her. Then there was another lady, Mindy, who was much younger and was technically one of our babysitters. She took care of us for a little bit while Luther was working, and she began to like him. Then there was another black lady, Cynthia, who also babysat us, and we would stay at her house if Luther got off late. She had a son, whom my brother and I got along with. Our original babysitter, Mindy, ended up joining us on our little family getaway to Lake Michigan.

He continued to keep me on my toes because I kept waiting for him to revert into the guy he was at the other apartments, but he didn't. We still got a whipping every now and then, but it wasn't a daily occurrence, and it didn't seem like it was with malicious intent.

When we arrived at the beach, we didn't seem to account for the weather very well because it began to rain so hard. My siblings and I were ready to get in the lake, but the rain hit our bodies like we were being struck by pellet gun bullets. My siblings and I raced to the car to find shelter, and our trip ended up being cut short. We grabbed some White Castle and headed back to our home.

When we got back, it was clear to see that Laurie was not impressed that Mindy got to go on the family trip with us. And that started a big confrontation that I think Luther wasn't ready for, but he must've been expecting it because he was the center of it all. I can't speculate if he was cheating on these ladies with each other, but I do know that they weren't upset at him for no reason.

This new home continued to be more stable and calm, unlike those horrible days in Willowbrook. I was starting to forget that, just a little while ago, I was crying my eyes out because I didn't want to come. I got to see this charm that Luther presented in court. School was just as normal. The mentoring program helped me get to know other students in the school. I made friends and got fairly comfortable there. I didn't get picked on much because some of the friends I had were older, and people knew not to mess with me.

I also decided to join the band. People gave you a hard time for being a "band geek," but I wasn't concerned with that. I was fascinated with music, and I wanted to learn how to play the alto saxophone. As I tried to break out my used alto saxophone from the school, it wouldn't play properly, so the teacher had to send it in to get serviced. It was going to take a few weeks, so she gave me the option to wait or learn another instrument, and I ended up picking the baritone tuba. I was the only one in class who was playing it, so that was why I chose it. It just looked cool to me, and I learned how to play it well.

I was adjusting well to this new life. I had a new school, new neighborhood, and unexpectedly a rehabilitated stepdad. I was starting to think I could live a life of stability away from my granny's house. Little did I know this happiness I was starting to experience would not last much longer.

One day I got home late from school, and I could not get in because no one was there. I ended up walking to a neighbor's house until someone picked me up. It turned out that Luther was arrested again, and we were about to move—only this time all five of us wouldn't be together. My baby sister and I went to stay with Granny again. My other two sisters and brother went to stay with their dad's sister. Luther's sister was asked why she didn't want to take in all of us, and she said that I wasn't his son and that my little sister was too young. The five of us would not live together again.

CHAPTER 14

Mercy

Grandma welcomed us back into her home with open arms. I expected nothing else. At this point, I was excited to be back at her house because there was so much stability tied to living with her. But there was a piece of me missing because of not being able to see my other siblings as frequently as I wanted. As time went on and we continued to adjust, I began to not experience things with my siblings the same way, and it wasn't the same when we were around one another. We went from seeing one another every day to not knowing what to do whenever we visited one another. It was like seeing a long-lost friend, and I felt like this toward my siblings, my flesh and blood.

I ended up back at Kingston Middle School, the school I was slated to go to before we moved back with Luther. That was a tough transition because I was just starting to get comfortable at Lakeland, but just like most of my life, change was bound to come. I went through the motions the rest of that sixth-grade year because I didn't want to get comfortable if things were just going to change on me. It seemed to be a blur as the school year finished.

At the start of the summer, my mentor put on the Ironman Golf Tournament, where a lot of older black men would come and participate. I don't think I realized the enormity of having that many prominent black men in one place. I literally saw what was possible for me when a lot of kids my age didn't have those positive role models. I wasn't intuitive enough to understand the magnitude of it.

I had to be out in the sun all day and help at this event. The best part about it was that I got to ride the golf carts as part of my job. When I had to drive to certain holes and put out advertisement signs, I also went around to offer drinks to the players while they were playing. In my clumsiness, I ended up breaking a winner's trophy, so he had to replace that one. He wasn't happy with me. In fact, he still reminds me about it. I helped my mentor with this tournament for the next couple of years. I didn't mind giving him a hand because he was so beneficial to my life. He also hooked me up with either goodie bags or cash, which didn't hurt.

Luther wasn't in jail for long, but we continued to stay with Granny. We did visit him at his new lady's house, who happened to be the same family friend we stayed with when he got arrested after the house fire. Her husband had passed away, and Luther, being the shady friend that he was, swooped right in to be with her. Luther was a cold piece of work. He had no chill at all. She had split up with her husband shortly before he passed, and she and Luther started dating soon after the breakup. We went to visit him on the weekends, all of us, so we were together at those times.

The house had three bedrooms and a huge basement. She had three daughters, whom I thought were pretty attractive. All but one of them were too old for me, but that didn't mean my mind wasn't thinking about what was possible. I was a twelve-year-old boy entering the puberty stage, and I was already exposed to sex.

We spent a good amount of time at that house in the summer before the school year began. My brother and I played the new *Need 4 Speed* game on the PlayStation. Luther even had the steering wheel to make it seem like you were really driving, but those never seemed to get you the control you have with an actual car.

We occupied our time carefully, but I really tried to get the youngest sister, who was a couple of years older than me. She never paid me any mind. Her favorite thing to say to me was "Boy, stop." I was persistent, to no avail. She either wasn't trying to get caught or genuinely wasn't feeling me. I chose to believe the former.

It seemed that "nice" Luther was starting to get back to his old ways. No one wanted to upset or frustrate him, and everyone seemed to walk cautiously around him. But that didn't work. Luther began to hit his new lady, but she wasn't letting him get away with that, and he ended up leaving and later going to jail. Fortunately, that was the last time we would live or visit with him. We went back to our respective housing: my youngest sister and I with Granny, and my three middle siblings with their aunt.

Before the summer ended, I was selected to be in the Pathfinder program at Indiana University Bloomington. This was my second time on the historic campus, and this time, I was getting a chance to experience it from the perspective of a college student. Four of us got to go from our town, and we instantly became a clique. Pathfinder was a program that allowed for middle school students to get a taste of what it would be like to attend college. The program didn't cost anything, and it ended up being really fun.

We stayed in and got a chance to experience the dorm, but my favorite part was that we got to eat at the dining halls. They were all-you-can-eat dining halls that cooked up some pretty tasty food; at least it was tasty for a middle schooler. I was on cloud nine. I ended up forging a bond with the people I came down to IU with. We also had a chaperone, who adored us. She was so awesome and did a great job of showing us what the campus had to offer. We visited museums and classrooms, played basketball, went swimming, and flirted with girls, of course. It was a dream. It was yet another opportunity to experience college life.

At this point, there wasn't any doubt in my mind that I was going to college, and I was intent on going to IU. It was one of the few campuses I visited, but I was establishing such great memories there. I left the Pathfinder program that year inspired and uplifted, ready to continue my trek toward college. As we left, I gave my chaperone a big hug and told her goodbye. We would keep in touch through e-mail, and she continued to encourage me when I needed it. I was ready for the school year to begin.

I began seventh grade in the same school where I finished sixth grade. School was school, but the bullying started to ramp up again. I was short, and I had bags under my eyes, which made me a prime target for my bully culprits. I was called so many names, but the main ones were Sleepy, Baggy, and Bag Lady. The kids would also tell me to get some sleep and that I looked like someone beat me up. It also didn't help that my granny didn't believe in shopping for name brands. We had to wear generic clothing and cheap nonbrand shoes.

When it was winter, you were cool if you had on some Timberlands. One time Granny got me knockoff Timberland boots. Timberlands have the famous tree logo on the side of the boots. Granny bought me some boots that had a mountain on the side of them. I knew what I was in for—a hell of a joinin' session. I tried to have my pants hide the logo, to no avail. They saw it, and they were relentless. I was embarrassed and angry that Granny would buy these, and I wanted to be anywhere but in that school.

It was so bad that I didn't wear those things again, and I opted to wear regular shoes while walking in a foot of snow to the bus stop. I would rather be cold as hell than be picked on for having knockoff Timberlands. When Granny found out I was walking outside in the cold without my boots, she lashed out at me, saying I was crazy and that I shouldn't listen to them. I knew she was right, but that didn't make the bullying stop.

There were only two of us staying at Granny's this time. My aunt Maya was less irritable, and the elder aunt, Sherrie, had moved out with her husband. I did what was asked of me. I had no interest in giving Granny a hard time. I would come home from school, do my homework, and head over to the Center. I was back hanging with my best friend Stephan, and even though we didn't go to the same school, we would always hang out anytime we were both at the Center. I was looking out for him, and he was looking out for me.

At the Center, I continued to go to mentoring with Mr. Hayes and the Stop the Madness program, but I established a solid relationship with my mentor. He was becoming more like a father figure to me. He checked on me all the time, and his number was etched in my brain. I called him often, and he made himself available to me no matter what he had going on. He taught me how to play golf, took me places like the movies, and many other things. Mind you, he worked full time, was a city councilman, and did so much for the community.

I bragged about my mentor often. I didn't know why he cared so much or why he was so invested in me, but I wasn't about to question it. He literally opened my world to new and better things, and he sparked the idea of college and opportunities for me. I saw more of the world in the short time since moving from my mom and Luther than I did my entire life.

School continued to be the same. I didn't run cross-country or play football; instead, I waited to run track in the spring. I was involved with the band, and my band teacher just so happened to coach our school's unofficial indoor soccer team, so I decided to join. I wasn't that good, but I made the most of it. We had an eighth grader on the team who was really good, and he would score all the goals. Since I would not get too many chances to score goals, I made it a point to rough up players against the glass wall of the indoor soccer field. I got a couple of yellow cards, but my teammates had my back if anybody got upset about me pushing them against the wall. We didn't win any championships, but it was cool to be part of that team.

That wasn't the first team I joined. There was a local football team that practiced right around the corner from our house. It was the Metro Raiders, and it was my first time being part of a team. That wasn't the best experience. The Metro League played all its games every Saturday at a middle school that didn't have a football team. The league included the Raiders, Rams, Redskins, Steelers, 49ers, and Titans. We came to really dislike the Rams because they usually beat everyone when they played. They always had teams that were bigger and faster than everyone, or at least it seemed like it.

At practice, I developed a fear of being hit. For whatever reason, I was one of the best players in my neighborhood; but when it came to having on pads, I was scared to hit and be hit. I did the conditioning and everything else, but I could not hit with pads. Whenever we did hitting drills, I tried to avoid it by skipping out on practice because I hated that part of it so much. There was one drill where they had a player in the middle of a circle shuffling his feet, and the coach would call out a number, and that person would go after the person in the middle. I think my teammates picked up pretty quickly that I was scared, so I was always an easy target. I developed the nickname of Gimpy. They made me dislike football, yet I kept coming back for more mainly because Granny made me, and she didn't want me to quit. I loathed going to every practice; it was becoming quite the chore. I was no good to the team and would never get playing time.

At one practice, I got pretty frustrated, and I decided that I wasn't going to take any crap. I was on the defensive scout team, and I knew the play that was about to be run. The wide receiver caught the ball, and I lit him up with a tackle—my best tackle of my young football career. I surprised everyone, especially the coach, who was thoroughly impressed. The wide receiver was not happy, and he and the quarterback conspired to jump on me after practice because they didn't like the hit. I thought it was worth it. It was the first time on the football field that I got props, and it felt good.

Seventh grade continued to move along. I only got into trouble a couple of times. I did get suspended from school a couple of times as well. The first time, I was coming back from lunch, and I decided that it would be a good idea to take the hat off a guy in my class who was much stronger than I was, and he beat me up. When I was in the office and the principal was talking to us, I ended up getting suspended from school. I was appalled at the fact that I got beat up in front of a lot of people and I still got suspended. Granny was upset at me, and I ended up being on punishment.

Later in the school year, my dumb decision making continued. There was a rumor that our school would be shot up on a specific day. I am not sure if we believed that would happen, but everyone took proper precautions as the day approached. There was a girl in my class whom I didn't particularly care for, and I decided that it would be cool to say that whoever was going to shoot up the school was going to shoot her. As I walked away laughing, thinking that I had "told her," I thought that was the end of it.

I was in my class later in the day and was summoned to the office. I didn't know what it was about, but I was becoming accustomed to going to the office. When I arrived, I found the girl and her friend in there, crying and sad. I knew what this was about, and the real question was how it was going to affect me. The principal explained to me that it was a big deal and that if I had any details about the rumor, then I should share, but I had no idea who the heck even made the threat. I tried to explain that it was a joke and that I didn't mean anything by it, to no avail. I was suspended from school for five days—five long days of no school because of a dumb thing I said. My granny was pissed. She whipped me, and I was suspended on top of that. I was really upset that I got suspended for something so stupid, but I had to suffer the consequences.

Eventually, I began to hang out with my new best friend Keon, who was a short guy but was packed with energy. No matter how short he was, this dude got mad respect from people in the neighborhood and school. Nobody would ever test him because he was crazy. I, Keon, and another friend, Ricky—who had a twin sister—all hung out outside and in school. I didn't see Stephan as much because not only did we not go to the same school but he also wasn't going to the Center as much anymore.

Keon and Ricky got me into some adventures. There were days when we would miss the bus and would have to walk to school. We mostly walked without getting into mischief, but we were young middle school boys and didn't know any better. When we were close to getting to school, we stopped at Burger King to get ice water or food if we had money. I still can't figure out how we didn't get the police called on us because we looked like we needed to be in school, but we weren't.

When we finished our ice water, we got this great idea to use the leftover ice and cup as an ice bomb. When we went into the neighborhood that was close to our school, we threw our cups of ice at people's cars and then ran. We ended up being successful until, one day, someone saw us and chased us in their car until we got to school. Of course, I was scared and didn't want Granny to find out I was doing this, so we tried to apologize for being stupid. Luckily, he showed mercy and didn't tell on us. We did not do that again for obvious reasons.

CHAPTER 15

Euphoria

I didn't really attract much attention from girls. It turned out that the bags under my eyes really pushed most girls away from me. I was always nice to girls, so I ended up being in the friend zone a lot. Kelly, whom I picked on when we were in third grade and whose brothers intended to beat me up but attacked my friend instead, began to be friendly with me. I wrote her notes on notebook paper and folded them up all special, and we would write back and forth. Nothing came of it, but it was interesting how that came full circle.

I did, however, meet a girl who would become my girlfriend. Her name was Bianca. She was new to our school, so she didn't necessarily know my history, and she didn't have any reason not to be with me. She thought I was cute, and I thought she was attractive, and we would talk and write letters. She was slightly taller than me, and she played on the basketball team. We dated for a couple of weeks, and then she broke up with me.

One day on our way home on the bus, I was minding my own business. Bianca, who was now my ex, decided that it would be cool to pick on me. I wasn't in the mood to be bothered by her, and she wasn't necessarily my favorite person because, after she broke up with me, I heard rumors that she started seeing other guys, and I felt like she had been playing me when we were together. As the ride continued, she berated me by constantly punching me in my arm and head. Frustrated, I told her to stop messing with me, and she continued. I then grabbed her and held her down in the other seat and told her to stop it. She agreed, so I let her go. As soon as I let her go, she started punching me in my face. I defended myself, and to this day, it is the only time I put my hands on a girl or lady in a malicious manner.

Bianca had a big brother who was in eighth grade. He was big for an eighth grader—six feet two inches and more than two hundred seventy-five pounds. I think he was held back. He heard the commotion in the back of the bus and rushed back to protect his sister. He threw me off and held me down, and his sister got one good hit in before the fight was stopped.

The bus driver finally realized that there was a lot of commotion in the back and stopped the bus. We talked it down like nothing was going on, so we didn't get in trouble for it. I was surprised that Bianca's brother didn't kick my butt. I was being watched over that day. As I got off at my bus stop, my friends pumped me up by saying that I kicked her butt, but I didn't look at it like that. I developed this idea that it wasn't right to put your hands on women, and I felt dirty because of it. It wasn't anything that I felt comfortable bragging about, even if she was taller than me.

Bianca and I ended up squashing the beef, but her friend tried to persuade her that she should beat me up. I told her that I wasn't down to fight her again because I didn't want to in the first place. That crisis ended up being averted.

Another person that I hung out with while I stayed at my granny's house the second time around was my cousin Kevin. I always had fun when I hung out at his house. His mom had worked at a big company for years, and she was making a good amount of money. They moved into this new house that was built from the ground up. It was the closest thing to a mansion to me, but it was so nice, and it smelled like it was brand new when I first started visiting. I tried to go over there as often as possible because we played his video games and various sports outside in his neighborhood, which had a bunch of other kids around our age. It was like a kid's paradise. We even ate well while we were over there, and we were up at all hours of the night.

The first time I stayed over there, it was for his twelfth birthday. He was a year younger than me. I was nervous because I didn't know his friends, but it was a ritual for him to have a sleepover every year for his birthday. The most fun thing that we did was play hide-and-seek in the dark. There was nothing like hiding and trying not to be it. That was like the highlight of the night because there were so many people playing, and his mom just let us have the house to do everything but tear it down. I went over to his house often and ended up establishing a great friendship with him.

At his house one day, he asked me if I ever jacked off. Granted, I had known about sex and thought I wasn't a virgin, but it turned out it was only what was considered dry humping, genital-to-genital action. When I got older, I figured out that wasn't considered sex. I had been desensitized to sex and wanted to do various things with girls, but I had never tried masturbation. When he explained what it was and that he would watch pornography before he did it, a whole new world opened up for me that I wasn't ready for. All the pain and agony that I suffered while growing up, coupled with messing around with older girls when I was younger, made me ripe to try something that would make me feel good. And boy, did I like that rush. When I tried it for the first time, it was like the greatest feeling in the world. I knew I had to experience that again, and that opened Pandora's box.

I ended up being addicted to masturbation and pornography. There was a difference between doing it just to have fun and "let one loose" and having a problem. One time I was so ready to masturbate that I did it in a golf course restroom. Every time I did it, I felt relief. It was like the feeling crackheads get when they first insert the needle into their skin. It was euphoria. I can imagine that most guys felt this way when they did it, but my situation was different because it became a way for me to relieve stress and get into a happy place. I guess it was better to do that than have sex, but it was something that I was really struggling with until I got older. I don't think Granny knew I was doing it as much as I was because I tried to hide it from most people. I began to regret learning about it from my cousin because it really consumed me at times.

As seventh grade continued, my grades were constant, and my behavior started to improve. I stopped doing stupid things for the most part. My mom was out of jail, and we visited her, or she would come by and visit us. We mostly visited her at her halfway house. Ms. Violet was the lady in charge, and she was a good woman. My mom was busy trying to get back on her feet. She was going to church and trying to get a job and a car. Ms. Violet set her up with a company that ended up giving her a car. There were times when Mom seemed frustrated by her situation, and then there were times when she was completely grateful for what was done for her.

Whenever we would stay at her house, my siblings would join us. All five of us were back together again to stay the weekend with her. I was in this weird state of mind where I was feeling uncomfortable staying there. I don't know what that was about. Maybe I wanted Mom to prove herself. Maybe I couldn't accept her back into our life. I mean, life was already unstable at times, and I was so used to being happy instead of having life change quicker than a pitch. I was apprehensive.

Mom was so proud of the kids we were becoming. We were growing up and turning into intelligent youngsters. When we were younger, she had us perform songs in front of her friends. She requested that my sister and I perform for Ms. Violet and the other women of the shelter. My eldest sister and I stood at the top of the stairs as if we were on a stage. She wanted us to sing "When You Believe" by Whitney Houston and Mariah Carey. We sang the heck out of that song. Everyone was so impressed. We felt good that day.

Back at Granny's house, it was business as usual. We still went to church, and this time around, they created a teen/young adult choir. I was put in the tenor section by default, and I immediately felt uncomfortable. I informed the choir director that I felt more comfortable singing higher and tried soprano. We realized that was too high, so we settled on alto, and that worked out best.

I really enjoyed myself singing in the choir, and my mom even got the chance to hear me sing one Sunday. It was good singing for the Lord, but I loved the attention I got because of it. I wanted so badly to sing lead on a song, but I never got the opportunity. There was one time when I was going to step in and sing for one of the choir members who had a lead, but we never sang the song. I was frustrated and threw a fit because I really wanted to sing lead, but apparently, it was for all the wrong reasons. I also tried to play the drums but never got good enough to play them consistently.

I also liked the idea of being a preacher. I would come home after church and look up scriptures and come up with sermons that went with them. One time when I went to church with my aunt Perla, we were attending the Wednesday night service. Out of boredom of being at her church, something I never told her, I started looking up scriptures and coming up with sermons. She saw me and felt the need to share it with the whole church, so I had to share the scriptures and the sermon titles. It was cool.

I knew she wasn't doing it because she was interested in what I came up with. She was only concerned with showing off her nephew to the church so she could look good. I didn't like her much, but I was forced to be around her. As soon as I was able to avoid her, I did. She just wasn't a nice person, and I didn't like going over to her house.

Life at the Center continued to be the same. I hung with my friends, and we continued to get into mischief. We once stole a bike, and I rode it around like it was nothing. I didn't always steal things, but they encouraged me to do so. My friend Keon didn't have a rough home, at least from my perspective. He was like me. He was the eldest of his siblings. He took care of them and made sure that nobody messed with them. He was just as overprotective of them as I was with my siblings, especially my little sister. He had a big house, and his mom worked a lot. We hung out there when she wasn't there. I don't think we were bad kids, just bored mostly and intrigued by the slight thrill of possibly getting into trouble. I had slight anger issues, but I was never really defiant in that sense. We were just trying to find something to do.

My relationship with my younger sister Lexus began to grow. I mean, there wasn't any doubt that she got on my nerves, but I loved her dearly. She was the only one of my siblings who lived with me. I was her big brother, and I had to make sure to watch over my little sister. Even though I went to school and on my little adventures after class, I made sure to keep a watchful eye on her. I had to beat up a few people to make sure they knew not to mess with her again.

When she first learned to ride a bike, she was outside riding one of the neighbor's bicycles, and my granny wanted me to get her because it was time for dinner. She would not come in because she was so excited about riding this bike. She must've felt exhilarated because I was not able to get her to obey. I had to chase her down, and finally, I was able to catch her but not before the bike fell on my leg and gave me a huge gash on my ankle. I started bleeding really bad, and I was so upset at her. I grabbed her so we could go in the house. I still have the scar on my leg, and every time I look at it, I am constantly reminded of that day. It is a special scar because it looks like I was clawed by a tiger.

That was really the only time when we clashed like that. She was hardheaded, and it was hard to keep up with her at times, but I wouldn't have had it any other way because that was my baby sister. She was all I had at that point, and I wasn't about to let anything ruin that.

CHAPTER 16

Mentors

There was another friend whom I got really close with in our neighborhood, and his name was Owen. He lived across the street from my granny. He had a lot of siblings, like me, and he was the eldest. We got along great. Whenever I hung out with him, we either played sports or video games. His mom was superstrict though. I knew how to shape up quickly whenever I was over there.

Owen played baseball with the local Little League. The Little League played all their games at the Weston Park baseball field, the same park that the Center was in. While he played in the game, his mother worked the concession stands. I went to watch him play often, but one day she asked me if I could help her out. I said sure, and I helped make items such as hot dogs and popcorn, and it was cool to be involved. She also paid me in chips, a drink, and a hot dog; and that, to me, was as good as being paid in cash.

I enjoyed watching the game so much that when a new team was being formed, I decided that I would give it a shot. We didn't need tryouts because we had just enough players to form the team. I wasn't any good because I had never played before, and that was the case for most of the other boys on the team. My old best friend Stephan was also on the team, which filled the void of Owen being on another team. We practiced and got positions and were excited going into our first game.

We ended up getting beaten badly. Then the next game came, and we lost again. I didn't like this feeling because I really didn't like to lose in anything. There was something frustrating about being on this baseball team, and I hit an all-time low of poor sportsmanship.

The position that I played on the team was first baseman, which I grew to love and was excited about. During one of the games, while we were already losing, the coach decided to move me to shortstop. I didn't know any better because some of the best baseball players were shortstops, but that didn't stop me from having a temper tantrum. As I got in the position, it just so happened that there was a ball hit toward me; and in my anger and frustration, I let it go right past me. I looked at the coach, and he was pissed, but the amazing thing about him was that he didn't yell at us in a malicious manner. He remained calm, and I had every reason to be yelled at that day.

I ultimately quit the team, but it was something that I should've learned from because that was so immature of me to be that way. Baseball could've been a sport that I grew to love had I stuck to it. After quitting the team, I realized that, going forward, I should not quit, and I should be a good teammate.

My mentor continued to be involved in my life. He was always checking on me, and I was constantly calling him to see when he would be available to meet up. One day he asked me to go to the movies with him to watch *Drumline*. That movie was great. We also continued to work on my golf game. I wasn't a young Tiger Woods, but I could hit the ball at least. I was too impatient at first to really learn golf, but it sparked enough interest that I kept playing periodically. I still play today. My mentor was a fairly good player, and I aspired to be as good or good enough to hold my own on a Saturday or Sunday morning.

The caseworkers kept making an appearance. At this point, I was growing tired of having these visits with them. They proved that they didn't have our best interests at heart when they moved us back with Luther, and I was starting not to trust them. We battled back and forth about my not wanting to even meet with them because I felt like it was pointless. My life was essentially as good as it had ever been, and I needed it to stay that way. I didn't believe that was too much to ask, and they shouldn't have either.

We also went to court on occasion. We had to go for updates about our parents and their status of getting us all back. We went enough to know patterns and people and what room was what in the courtroom. It was too many times for any kid. The best part about it was that all my siblings were reunited, so it turned out to be a mini–family reunion. Don't get me wrong; I didn't have mean caseworkers, but I was obviously turned off by that decision to move us, and then we ended up back where we started. I wasn't going to allow my voice to go unheard, but I also was going to prevent getting close to them until they proved themselves.

At school, things continued to flow. I started to get ready for track season, which I was superexcited for. I had a failed attempt at cross-country in sixth grade, but I was ready to prove how fast I could run and how far I could jump. I was always fairly athletic, but I didn't always show up when it was necessary, such as when I was on the baseball and football teams. But track was another beast. I enjoyed that because there wasn't contact. You were also primarily by yourself, and there wasn't much difficulty involved in it; you just ran as fast as you could.

As we started to train, they wanted us to have our physicals done, and Granny brought me. I had complained about a knee issue. It was sore, and I had a slight bump beneath my knee. It turns out I had a condition called Osgood-Schlatter disease, a growth disorder that affects the knees, usually in children who participate in sports that involve running and jumping. I was told it would go away on its own, but the doctor said if it was bothering me, then I should not run until it got better. I was so disappointed that I wished I hadn't said anything because Granny was not about to let me run track because of doctor's orders. Best believe I didn't complain to her about soreness again. I didn't want to experience not being allowed to continue playing sports.

As the season went on, I went out and supported the team anyway. There was a relay that was specific to sixth and seventh graders called the sprint medley. They competed at the varsity level, but no eighth graders could be on it. It consisted of the one hundred meters, two hundred meters, and four hundred meters. A different athlete would do each distance, with the exception of two runners doing one hundred meters. Our relay team was decent, but as I found out, it was missing a pivotal piece.

My coach, who was also my PE teacher, approached me about working on my grandma to let me run just that one race. My knees weren't hurting, and I felt like I could do it. My coach didn't say why she wanted me in the race, though, so I insinuated that the first leg was too slow and that she needed me because I was faster, but Granny wasn't having it. She kept saying that it was doctor's orders and that I could not run.

My cousin Daniel was having a birthday sleepover; these seemed to be the thing to do for birthdays. He was the one who got in trouble with my brother and me for stealing the money from the Center. He lived around the corner from us, so I was excited to go. We lived close, but we didn't hang out as much as we probably could have. When I went over there, there were other boys. I only knew my other cousin Kevin. There was food, and he had a PlayStation, and *Tony Hawk's Pro Skater* was the game of choice.

The night was going well until my cousin decided to bully me. I am not sure why I was the target, probably because I was an easy one, but I was going to defend myself in any situation. My guard was always up. All of those years of whippings and beatings from Luther forced me to have heightened senses. I am not sure what sparked it, but he tried to punk me, and the other boys were definitely instigating the situation. I don't remember where my cousin's mom was, and his dad didn't live there.

I believe we were home alone, or his elder sister was watching us (but not paying attention). It got to a point where we were fighting, throwing punches back and forth. I was angry that I was even put in this situation, and the birthday boy was trying to prove to his friends he could fight. Someone broke the fight up, and all was calm. We ended the night by watching *Leprechaun*. That movie was trippy.

The next morning, the boys continued to aggravate the situation between my cousin and me, and we ended up having round two. The consensus was that I won the fight. I think my cousin was frustrated because he was bigger than me yet couldn't beat me up. I felt good, but it wasn't a win if I was fighting my cousin for no good reason. Nevertheless, I was going to take this confidence and roll with it. I felt good, nonetheless, that I stood my ground, and I created quite the reputation in my family that I wasn't one to play with.

In my neighborhood, I didn't walk around like I could whip anybody, but I also stood up for myself. One day one of the kids in my neighborhood got boxing gloves, so some of us went over to his house to try them out. He decided that he wanted to box me. I was an easy target because I was short, so everyone thought they could punk me, but I wasn't backing down. I grabbed my boxing gloves and put them on. Then it was fight time. I gave him a combo he couldn't recover from, and I ended up winning the match. He wasn't too happy and wanted to fight me without the gloves, but I knew if I beat him with gloves, then I could defeat him without them. We never fought again.

I would still hang out with Keon and Ricky but mainly with Keon when Ricky couldn't hang. We got into some good adventures. On one of our escapades of roaming the neighborhood, I found out that my biological dad's grandmother lived close by. Once I found that out, I visited her whenever I was in her neck of the woods. My grandpa lived there, so I would see him, and I was able to meet my uncles. I also got a chance to see my dad and be introduced to some of my siblings on my dad's side, whom I never met before.

I knew of my dad and met him a couple of times before, but we didn't have a close relationship. Whenever he was there, we would hang out and play video games. He had a Dreamcast, and we would play *NBA 2K* together. He wouldn't let me win; he was just as competitive as I was. That must've been where I got it from. It was cool to be hanging with my dad like that. I think I was in a place of not being able to really accept people into my life because of the instability that was ever present. I let myself stay in the moment.

My dad's grandmother was the sweetest. She was the same every time I came over. She usually was watching television, and whenever I came over, she would show me pictures of when I was a kid. If I needed it, she gave her last bit of money to make me happy. The great thing about her was that she did that for any of her many grandkids and kids. She was a beautiful soul that I grew to love, despite my recent apprehension to getting close to folks. She was one of the few people in my life who was there when I needed her, and I could always count on her to be smiling anytime I came by to see her.

As I continued to visit every now and then, my dad would be either there or gone. If he wasn't there, I hung out with my great-grandmother and watched television with her. It was that time that I cherished and didn't mind spending time out of my little adventures to hang with her.

CHAPTER 17

Bittersweet

Every now and then, we went to stay with my aunt Cece, who lived next door to where Luther used to live with his ex-girlfriend. She took care of us when my granny had to work late. We also went to her church. She had two daughters and a son. Her son, Matt, took me in as his little brother. I was always trying to follow him around. He was in college and then ended up coming back home. We played video games together and went to the local park to shoot hoops. He also cut my hair whenever I needed.

The activity that I enjoyed the most while hanging out with him was going to the mall. I loved going to the mall. We wouldn't even buy anything besides food in the food court. We literally went to the mall and walked around, just hanging out. The one thing we made a ritual of was going in each of the shoe stores to see what shoes were on sale. It was such a small activity, but I looked forward to it every time. I window-shopped because my grandmother never bought me name-brand stuff, and I wanted it so kids would stop making fun of me. My cousin gave me a pair of his Nikes that were a little too big for me, but I wore them until I couldn't wear them anymore. They weren't even a solid color, but I didn't care; it was name brand.

One day the unexpected happened. My granny brought us to Value City, which was a department store. We were there shopping for new shoes because I was due. She normally picked the shoes out for me to make sure they were in the budget. She ended up picking out a pair of K-Swiss. I lit up as I rushed to try them on. I tried to pretend like they were the perfect fit, but they were actually a bit too small. I decided to go ahead and get them because they were name brand, and Granny had never bought me one before. She was all-in this time, though. My granny was about to buy me my first pair of name-brand shoes. I was in heaven, and I wore those shoes until my granny had to throw them out.

Granny didn't really give us an allowance, but I did have an opportunity to make a little money. I started helping at a barbershop that was walking distance from our house. I went in early on Saturday mornings and helped sweep and do whatever was needed. The owner paid me $5 and sometimes gave me a free haircut. Once again, I was surrounded by positive black men who would ultimately inspire me to see myself in a greater light than society saw me.

I also got a chance to work with one of the other mentors from the Stop the Madness program who owned an auto-repair shop—another black man owning a business. I helped him clean up and move things, and I even cut the grass with his John Deere riding mower. He paid me $10 to $20, depending on the level of work I put in. I didn't realize the magnitude of all this influence in my life, but it ultimately shaped me into the man I am today.

He also brought me somewhere that would change my perspective on people who were different from me. He frequented a community center that welcomed people who had disabilities. They let the people do different activities, including basketball. He asked me if I wanted to go, and I said sure.

When I got there, I didn't think less of them, but I did automatically think that I was going to be better than everyone on the court. Boy, was I wrong! They could hang with the best of them, and I felt like an idiot because I thought that I would defeat them because they had disabilities. But I learned that they could compete with anyone, regardless of their disabilities, and I had no right to think that they wouldn't be capable of holding their own on the basketball court. It was almost like a lesson that he was trying to get me to learn, and once it dawned on me that these folks had game, I left that place realizing I could not judge folks because of their shortcomings. I needed to give everyone the benefit of the doubt.

As we left the building, we discussed what just happened, and he was happy to see that I had learned my lesson. To reward me for it, he found a coupon in the paper for a Lee's Famous Recipe Chicken meal. Lee's had chicken that would make you want to "slap your mama." It was better than any chicken chain you could think of. The only other chicken that was up to par with Lee's was my mom's. They also had delicious sides that complemented the chicken, and they had a biscuit that just melted in your mouth. I was so excited when we arrived at Lee's. We ended up getting a three-piece meal for $3.99. What a deal!

The foster care system was so annoying because of the many court dates. We had to miss a day or half a day of school, which I didn't necessarily mind, but I wasn't trying to spend it in court. My mom was in and out of possibly getting us back. She made promises often, and I believed her but only to a certain extent. I wanted to live with my mom, but I also enjoyed where we were living. My life had completely turned around, and we were experiencing things that I wouldn't have experienced if we had stayed with my mother and Luther.

Things were going well for her. She was clean, and she had a house that was down the street from my granny's house. We spent the night there to see what it would be like. The house was huge. It had four or five bedrooms, and the idea of still having my own room was enticing. There was something about it that made me apprehensive, though. We weren't rich at Granny's place, but being with her made it seem like we weren't poor. When we stayed at my mom's house, it just seemed like we would end up struggling again. Mom sensed that from me, and we conflicted on that. She broke down, saying that she was trying and to stick with her, but I wanted to wait and see what would happen.

Every other month, I went to visit my cousin Kevin. He was, for the most part, welcoming. We clashed every now and then, but it wasn't anything that ruined the friendship we had. One thing I did do was protect him. I made sure that nobody would mess with him on my watch.

One day I went over to his house, and he told me that there was a boy in the neighborhood messing with him. I confronted the kid and asked him why he was messing with my cousin, but he couldn't muster up any good answer. I told him to ensure that he didn't mess with him again, or I would be sure to show him what would happen if he did. He was intimidated and decided to get his cousin to come by and check me, and I wasn't backing down, so we ended up squashing the beef and moving on. I am not sure why I gained the reputation that I did. I believe it was because of the anger I was fostering that I never really got a chance to address.

Kevin and I also played a lot of sports. He had a basketball hoop in front of the house and a park across the street. We always had epic basketball games. I was as competitive as he was, so most of the time, we would be on different teams and add players to make it a challenge. I would win, and then he would win, and it would always be back and forth like that. We also played football. We got into some intense tackle football games. I mainly won those because I was much faster. All this activity kept us from gaining weight from all the food we ate.

We also got into some adventures. We walked to nearby places like Kmart to get snacks or to other people's houses. We played hide-and-seek one night with other kids from the neighborhood. We used the entire neighborhood as our hide-and-seek area. It was a quiet cul-de-sac with about ten houses. It made for epic games, and we had so much fun. We also came in late, but his mom would already be asleep. I really enjoyed going over there because we really had an opportunity to just be ourselves.

However, it wasn't all fun and games when I went over there. Kevin and I got into it often as most young boys of that age do. We butted heads either because one of us lost or because we did something to each other that we didn't appreciate. We never really fought, but it turned into me getting teased. I didn't always appreciate what he had to say because he would hit me where I was already sensitive—he talked about the bags under my eyes. When it really got bad, he and his fourteen-year-old sister, Ashley, would gang up on me, making me sad and ready to go home. Those were the times I didn't like being over there, but the fun that we had outweighed the bad times.

As time went on, my caseworker asked what I would like to do as far as my future home was concerned. Adoption was something that I was thinking about often. My mom wasn't going to get her rights back anytime soon, Luther was out of the question after he caught his last case, and my biological dad wasn't in any position to take me in either. One thing I did want was to not be in the system and not continue meeting with the caseworkers at the most inopportune times. Granny wasn't in any position to adopt us, so she supported my wish to get adopted. It had always been in the back of my mind, and I wanted that for myself and Lexus. My sister was too young to understand this because she essentially grew up with my granny. All she really knew was that Granny was our caregiver.

There never was any conversation about the adoption after that, until one day my caseworker approached us about moving into a foster home that could possibly turn into adoption. I wanted adoption, but I also loved living with Granny. However, it was becoming clear that Granny was getting older and that she wasn't going to be able to care for us like we needed. I was getting older and starting to explore things, and my little sister was becoming a riot as she got older. She was getting kicked out of preschool. We were becoming a handful, and I knew Granny was getting tired. I wasn't upset about this possibility because I felt like Granny put in her time. She did the best she could with what she had, and I am forever grateful. The caseworker was going to give us a preview visit, where we would spend the weekend at the foster home and see if we liked it. It was obviously bittersweet, but I knew it was needed.

The school year ended, and the idea of heading to eighth grade began to excite me. We always admired the eighth graders, and I looked forward to finally being one. I ended the year with good grades, which were never an issue, and that was a credit to numerous people, including my granny and my mentor. At the beginning of summer, my mentor enlisted my help with his golf tournament again. I was also on track to go back to the Indiana Black Expo. The Black Expo, this time around, was fun because I was older, and we could have more freedom. Instead of being forced to only do the conference and other obligatory activities, we could explore a little bit.

One time while in TJ Maxx, we spotted E-40 and followed him to his hotel. He gave us his autograph on a receipt and sent us on our way. I don't know what happened to it.

For the organized activity, we did something I was interested in—the UniverSoul Circus, a predominantly black circus crew that claimed to have the best circus show on the planet. It lived up to the billing. The circus was so fun and entertaining. They really put on a great show.

The one thing I wondered about the Black Expo was if those many black folks gathered in one place at one time could behave themselves. I don't ever remember feeling unsafe at the expo, nor do I remember any major violence happening. The police presence was there just in case, but people proved that they were down there to have fun, not start stuff. I can still hear the loud music playing from cars on the street, while some rude guys yelled from their cars at ladies walking on the sidewalk. Everyone and their mother were at this expo, and it was the thing to be part of every summer.

After I returned from the expo, it was time for my sister Lexus and me to go preview the new foster home. My sister was indifferent. I don't know if she was excited or just along for the ride, but I was nervous. I didn't know what to expect or where it would be, but it was going to be a new adventure. Our caseworker ended up driving us over there. This new family lived about fifteen to twenty minutes away.

As we arrived, we marveled at the beautiful home that must've been built within the previous five years. It was in a cul-de-sac neighborhood akin to my cousin Kevin's. They also had a basketball hoop in the front, so that really got me excited. We rang the doorbell, and a lady answered. Her name was Mrs. Williams. Her husband was on the couch. They were welcoming and warm. It was love at first sight.

It was a four-bedroom home with two and a half bathrooms. There was enough to fit two kids per room. Mrs. Williams had kids from a previous relationship, who lived at the home, two boys and a girl. I was to room with the youngest of the two boys, and my sister was to room with the girl. They also had another foster kid living there named Austin, who was going to the eleventh grade.

As we started to get more acquainted, the caseworker felt she could leave us there to explore. When she left, we were shown our rooms, and the fun began. We had access to video games, good food, and a basketball court; there were older boys to hang out with, and we swam at the pool in the apartment complex across the street. What more can you ask for in a place to stay?

My sister bonded right away with the girl in the house, so she was having a good time. When I hung out with the brothers, it was like they were recruiting me for the football team. They were telling me how cool it was to live there and how they would go to the mall to shop for school clothes, and I didn't need to hear any more after that. After years of being at Granny's and not being able to shop for name brands, I was so excited about being able to shop for school clothes—at the mall of all places.

I was really sold and so ready to move in. As the weekend ended, our caseworker arrived, and we both agreed that we wanted to stay there. The plan was put into motion to have us move in before the school year started. I don't know what was more alarming: the fact that I was so numb to having to move again or the fact that I would have to go to my third middle school in three years, the seventh school overall. That much moving is not healthy, but somehow I wore it as a badge of honor. I became accustomed to having to switch schools, make new friends, and start the endless process of happiness again because that's all every kid ever wants—to be happy.

As it came time to leave my grandmother's home, we packed our things and said goodbye to her, our friends, and the Center. I never attended the Center regularly again. I wouldn't get to see my friends whom I hung out with for a while. I was going to a new environment and new neighborhood. The new adventure for my sister and me awaited.

CHAPTER 18

New Beginnings

We arrived at the house again, hopeful that it would be as cool as our visit. Before we arrived, we found out that Mr. Williams was my biological uncle on my dad's side. He was my grandma's brother. They found out during a conversation about who was moving into the home. It was a crazy coincidence, but for me, it was a way of getting around the fact that I was living in a foster home. Instead of having to explain that to my nosy classmates, I just told everyone that I was living with my aunt, uncle, and cousins. Luckily for me, I didn't have to lie about that.

As we got ready to gear up for school, me in eighth grade and my sister in kindergarten, we each got to establish our own identities and make waves in our own lives. I ended up sharing a room with Derrick, who was tall and chill. He was going to the tenth grade. We got along well. His brother, Jacob—going to the eleventh grade—shared a room with Austin. They both were chill. My sister shared a room with Veronica, the younger sister of Jacob and Derrick. Their dad stayed in the apartments across the street, so they would go visit him often. I got along well with everyone in the house. I didn't foresee any issues.

Every day until the start of school, we would do something, whether it was playing basketball or swimming at the apartments; we didn't have time to be bored. If we had cash (we did get an allowance, which was completely foreign to me), we walked to the convenience store down the street to stock up on what we needed. We also hung out with Johnathon, who stayed in the apartments, as well as Drew and his brothers, who were from a different state. It helped that I had Derrick and Jacob to hang out with because they knew people, and they integrated me into the fold with ease. Drew ended up helping me at my new school since we were in the same grade.

Austin, the other foster youth, almost always did his own thing. He was three years older than me, and he was out and about a lot. He was really into cooking and wrestling. He wasn't into other sports. He rode his bike everywhere. He was always on the move. Whenever he was home, we bonded over the fact that we were both foster youth, and we both liked wrestling. His favorite wrestler was Stone Cold Steve Austin. He gave me some advice that threw me for a loop. He told me not to be fooled by the Williamses' niceties and that they would eventually show their true colors. He wanted me to just look out for myself and my sister when the time came. I had yet to see this, but it would surface as time went on.

The neighborhood was quiet and quaint. I would say it was a better neighborhood than my granny's. I never experienced any issues while I lived with Granny because we were pretty sheltered from the trouble that would occur over there. As we got signed up, I continued to find my way at my new school, Maytown Middle. It happened to be the rival school of my old one, Kingston. It seemed like I was just finishing sixth grade, and now I was finally the big man on the middle school campus as an eighth grader. However, that wasn't the truth. I had to find my way around as if I were a sixth grader again.

Drew made it easy for me by inviting me to eat lunch with him and his friends. He was one of the popular guys at the school. I ended up finding some friends whom I could vibe with in Ben, Sean, and Jason. These guys were a good group of friends whom I came to know well, Ben more so than the others. As classes went on, I continued to do well in school. I wasn't having any issues in the classroom. I did have trouble navigating the social scene. Between trying to get with girls and staying in with the cool crowd, I was trying to make it work.

I also stayed in band. I had been part of a band since sixth grade, and I figured I would do that instead of choir. I continued to play my baritone tuba, although I was very tempted to try a cooler different instrument, like the trumpet or the drums. I didn't want to be wishy-washy, so I stuck to what I knew. A female bandmate and I played the same instrument; it was safe to say I was better than her. I played the instrument really well, but the only thing I struggled with was reading the music. I would always mark my book up by writing the notes instead of seeing the notes and playing them. I did that because it was easier for me.

It came time for tryouts for the football team, and something in me wanted to try out and see if I could make it. We had the potential to be a good team, and I had been playing well in the neighborhood games, so I wanted to see what I could do. The tryouts lasted two days, and I made the team because I had one good play where I sacked the quarterback hard. He wasn't happy, but I was excited. That was my signature play that helped me make the team. I didn't get much playing time, though. I only got in when the game was out of reach, just like when I was younger, playing for the Metro Raiders. I was always good whenever I didn't play on an official team, but I had this mental barrier that I couldn't get over when playing with equipment.

We had a team that was loaded. This team was full of really good players all over the field: fast running backs, two talented quarterbacks, and a stifling defense. All three of my new friends played on the team, and it was fun. We ended up going undefeated and winning the city championship, beating Laney Middle School. My old friend Stephan played for that team.

We had haters on our way to the championship. When we played Gilroy Middle, they didn't necessarily like that we beat them the way we did. They wanted to fight us, so the coaches got us on the bus as quickly as possible. They tried to get us off the bus and fight, but the coaches weren't having it. That was the only issue we had as we steamrolled to the city championship. It was a fun season because that was the first championship team I was a part of.

At home, things were normal. We got meals every night, and things were going smoothly. There were incidents here and there, but nothing too crazy. The biggest issue I had was when my sister and Veronica would get into arguments or fights. I obviously couldn't really do anything about it because they were girls, but she was two years older and bigger than my sister, so my protective-brother instincts would kick in, and it would frustrate me that I couldn't do anything but listen to my little sister crying out loud. They always took Veronica's side too. Veronica blamed Lexus for everything. I don't know how much that affected my little sister, but I felt resentment.

Mr. and Mrs. Williams played favoritism often. It wasn't subtle either. Mrs. Williams would make it known that her kids got special privileges. She often made it a point to remind us that we were not hers and that her kids would often be a priority over us. That was when I really started to notice what Austin was talking about when he said, "Watch your back." I began to be cautious, and with every move and situation, I began to make more decisions for myself. This would grow over time, but it began later, during my eighth-grade year.

My relationship with the boys continued to be fine. I never had a problem with them because they were as chill as could be. We often shared clothes, so I would wear something of theirs every now and then, and they would borrow clothes from me as well. We continued doing that, and it was easy for me because people at school wouldn't see what they were wearing because they were in high school. Some of my friends noticed and would point it out, but I didn't get embarrassed about it.

Another thing that bothered me about Mrs. Williams was that she demanded that we call her Mom. This was tough for me because I was not comfortable with calling anyone Mom who wasn't my mother. Even though my mother wasn't in my life anymore, it wasn't like I hated her. I loved my mom. The situation that she got in was her fault, but she didn't get a fair shake because of the pain and strife that she had to endure in her life. The fact that I had to call Mrs. Williams Mom—and she didn't earn it—bothered me, but I knew that was the rule in her home, and I was willing to follow it no matter how frustrating it was to be calling her something she obviously was not. I struggled with calling her Mom at first, and I am sure she noticed it, but eventually, I just got over it.

I yearned to be part of another team, so when it came time to try out for the basketball team, I was all over it. I went to tryouts not necessarily expecting to make the team but definitely willing to give it a try. I had a good first day, and to my surprise, the next day, my name was on the list to come to the second day of tryouts. I tried my hardest, which consisted in playing well in the scrimmage portion, but I didn't do so well. I felt like the team was picked already and that the second-day invitees were only there to make us feel good. I didn't mind because I didn't expect to make the team because of my height.

I was cut, so I focused more on band. I was already in band class, and because of my being on the football team, I didn't have the obligation to participate in the required band activities outside class. I joined our pep band, which played at the basketball games. We played songs like "Tequila," "We Will Rock You," and "Star-Spangled Banner," just to name a few. That was fun to be part of because our basketball team was pretty good. We didn't end up winning the championship, but we were close. We really tried to sweep the main titles: football, basketball, and track and field. I loved that school because there was so much talent.

My relationships with girls at that school were better than I had before, but I still had my fair share of issues. I tried talking to a girl named Patricia; she was in choir. She was pretty. We exchanged letters, until one day I found out she was talking to one of the guys who talked to every girl he could, and I felt played. I confronted her by calling her a hoe, and all hell broke loose. Her friends got mad at me and tried to call me out. My friends just laughed at me and didn't try to help me at all. Those guys still laugh at me about that to this day.

Then I met Brooklyn, who was also in eighth grade. She was cute and tall. I liked her demeanor and the way she dressed, and we got along well. We called each other boyfriend and girlfriend and would exchange notes. We talked on the phone, and it was basically a school romance, until she decided that she didn't want us to be together anymore. I found out she was talking to someone else at another school, and I felt devastated. I didn't care for girls playing me like a fiddle, and I wanted to make sure that this would not happen again, so I lay low with the relationships after that and just focused on more important things. She tried to continue to play with my emotions up until high school. I ended up being her rebound, and I couldn't understand why I would not let her go.

My caseworker continued to check in on us and see how we were doing. The Williams family was always on par when it came to making sure we put on a good impression for the caseworker. I was content where I was, but I made it a point to let our caseworker know about my wishes to be adopted. She was a cool person, but I was tired of having her visit and being checked on like that. I was living a normal life by my standards, and I wanted to be able to not have to be observed by the state and the court.

I knew my mom wasn't going to bust through the doors and get custody of us. Mrs. Williams went out of her way to make sure we didn't have any contact with our mother. When my mom got out of jail, we saw her if we visited our sisters because they would coordinate it. My mom was still in communication with the family where Renee and Mercedes were staying. My brother, Luther Jr., was now living in a group home. Lexus was always in a bad mood when we came home from visiting my sisters. Once Mrs. Williams would see that, she would make it a point for us not to go over there, and my sisters really hated that about her. They despised Mrs. Williams, and she made sure to shelter Lexus from what she thought were negative influences on my little sister.

CHAPTER 19

Stitches

At school, things seemed to keep moving along. My grades continued to soar, and the girl drama was dissipating. But there was this one guy, who was the class clown, always making fun of me and my friends. I always made comments to people that I would kick his butt if it ever got down to it, and word got around that I was talking crap. We finally set it up to fight in the locker room during my PE class. His name was Gerald, and he just so happened to be the same person I threatened when we were younger in elementary. We were now in eighth grade, fourteen years old, and filled with adrenaline.

Gerald found his way to the gym, even though he wasn't in that class. We stood opposite each other, waiting to see who would make the first move. He did, and he got a good punch in. He hit me, and I staggered; then it was a battle. The fight was relatively even, until my friend Ben tried to break it up and got in the way, giving my opponent a free opportunity to punch me at will. He slammed my head against the wall, and that was that. The fight was over. I was left there with my friend Ben trying to gauge whether I lost the fight, and the look on his face confirmed that I did.

Drew came in after the fight and wanted to know what happened because he missed it. He hyped me up about a rematch, and I turned red. I angrily went after Gerald, who had left the locker room laughing and feeling confident, and I wanted to really hurt him, but I never got a chance.

After the fight, everyone said that I got beaten down, but the name-calling stopped. In my mind, I accomplished what I wanted. Drew tried to set up a rematch at his place, and I was down, but Gerald never showed up. I had it in my mind that since he stopped picking on us and he wasn't down to fight again, he knew that it wouldn't have the same result. I felt that if he were that confident that he could beat me up, then he would've accepted a rematch with no problem. That was my thinking, and it made me feel better after the fact.

The band was due for a big middle school competition, and the director wanted us to practice for it. He wanted us to make a great impression on the judges. We had some awesome pieces that we were working on, and he wanted to make sure that we were playing up to our ability so we could win the competition. We had some good rehearsals leading up to the competition, and he was feeling confident about our ability to do well.

On the day of the competition, we were on the bus on a Saturday. I sat in the back with Leo, who was the life of our band party. He was multitalented. He was in and out of the choir, and he played the drums and the trumpet. He made the trip fun as we laughed about all types of things.

When we got to the school where the competition was held, it was all business. I was ready to go and ready to help the band do well by playing my parts well. When it was our time, we played only for the judges. After we played, we all thought that it was great and waited to hear the results. We ended up getting a gold rating, which meant we did really well. Everyone was so excited and hyped. The band teacher was ecstatic and couldn't wait to get back to school and tell everyone.

Our band teacher read us the comments from the judges, and they made it a point to mention how well the baritone tuba players did. They said that we were strong and complemented the rest of the music well. It was a great feeling, and I really felt good because there were only two of us, and I was a much better player than the other. That was a good moment for me and our band.

After that, I knew I was going to Wayman High School the next year, and they were trying hard to get me to play when I got there, but I didn't want to. I didn't want to be considered a band geek, and I opted instead to play sports when I got to high school.

As basketball season concluded, I knew that I wanted to run track. It was always something that I had in my thoughts, and I hadn't had a chance to participate since sixth grade. I wasn't going to let anything or anyone keep me from running on the team this time around. As tryouts began, I gravitated to the hurdles. There were four of us who ran the hurdles. The other people were faster, but I wasn't slow. We did well and were on track to possibly win the championship, but we lost our dual meet to Laney Middle, who got revenge on us for beating them in the football city championship.

I competed until we got to the city league meet, where we faced all the middle schools in the school district. There were a limited number of hurdle race spots up for grabs for the championships, and I wasn't able to beat out my teammates for the spot. I didn't want to be left out, so I asked my coach about any event I could do instead, and she said the mile run. I had not run the mile all season, and I was a sprinter through and through. However, I really wanted to be with my team for the championship meet. I decided I would try, and they agreed, thinking I wouldn't make it past prelims.

When it came time to compete, I ended up taking the last qualifying spot, making it to finals. What happened after that was an embarrassment. I ended up coming in last at finals, and I vowed to never be in last place again. I upheld that vow until I got to college. We were the runner-up in the meet as our nemesis, Laney Middle, ended up winning the championship. They got the last laugh.

As the school year came to a close, there was an overnight sleepover at the school for the eighth graders. The night was cool. We did dodgeball and basketball, watched movies, and did other activities. The idea of being at school at night, free to roam around, was cool. All the cool kids who had girlfriends were looked at as the power couples. They found a room in the gym that was dark, and there were activities going on in there that I don't think any teacher would have approved of—or any parent for that matter. All I know is that I wasn't part of it, and I felt left out. I ended up playing basketball for most of the night with another kid in the school and left it at that.

My friendship outside school with Jason and Sean continued to bud into something. Every now and then, I would hang out with them, and it was fun times. One day I was with Jason, and I wanted to ride his uncle's moped, which he let Jason use. I thought it was cool, and I wanted so much to ride it. It was the weekend before Memorial Day, and he finally let me ride it at the house of another friend's girlfriend. We were jumping on her trampoline, and he finally gave in to letting me ride it in the neighborhood. At first, I drove up and down the neighborhood, and I got bored. Then I turned onto a major street and was fine.

I did it again, and this time, a car was behind me. I attempted to get out of the way, turning on the street I turned on before, but my hand was stuck on the gear, and I wasn't able to stop the moped. I ended up running right into a vacuum cleaner store, across the street from a grocery store. The moped hit a parking block, and I flew headfirst into the wall. I hit my head pretty hard, and blood started gushing from my head instantly. I tried to get up, pick up the moped, and go back like nothing happened because I knew I was in trouble, but an off-duty firefighter saw me crash and came over to help. He told me that I needed to lie down because I looked like I was hurting badly, and I needed an ambulance.

There I was, bleeding from my head to my left arm, staring at the blue sky with little clouds, analyzing the people trying to help me. The ambulance got closer and closer, and people came to my aid. I was so calm for a person who got into an accident, and I was sure to be in a lot of trouble. They asked me if someone could help me, and I mentioned that my friend Jason was around the corner.

Meanwhile, Jason and our other friends were joking around about what if I crashed as they heard the sirens. The man tried to call Jason, but he wouldn't answer until after a few tries. He finally came, and I told him I was sorry and that I hoped the moped was still drivable. He told me not to worry about it and that I just needed to get well. As I got in the ambulance, he called Mr. and Mrs. Williams, and my foster father met me at the hospital.

When I got there, they brought me to the room to assess the damages. I needed seven stitches in my head and five more on my arm. Once they stitched me up, I was experiencing little to no pain, and I was released to Mr. Williams, who came while Mrs. Williams stayed back with the kids. My pride was hurt; it was so embarrassing. I walked out into the lobby with my bloody Kentucky jersey and was met with looks from people wondering what happened to me.

When I got home, I rested. I thought I would be in big trouble, but they were just making sure I was okay. Once my friends knew that I was okay, the jokes started flowing faster than Niagara Falls. It didn't help that I ran into a vacuum cleaner shop. They called me all types of vacuum cleaners, and the big scar on my head would be a reminder of that day and a cue for my friends to have a good laugh.

The following Monday was Memorial Day, and the last day of school was near. The Williamses had paid for me to go with the eighth graders to Cedar Point. Mrs. Williams wanted me to check with the doctor to make sure it was okay for me to ride the roller coasters with stitches, and he said it was cool, but I would have to wear a Band-Aid over it. Here I was wearing a big Band-Aid on my forehead and a stocking cap to cover it up. Talk about being more embarrassed. I wasn't going to allow that to ruin my fun. I ended up having a blast at Cedar Point, riding some superfun rides. I got to bond with some of my classmates for the last time before summer vacation and the start of high school.

That summer was probably one of the best ones I ever had. It was the first time I went into a summer excited about what was next. During most of the summers leading up to this one, either I was angry that I was going to be home with Luther all summer or I didn't know if I would end up moving away to a different home. That summer was different in the sense that I wasn't going anywhere, and I had much to look forward to when going to high school. There was so much that I could do. We swam at the pools in the apartments across the street; I could kick it with my cousin Kevin, who lived close by; and I could hang out with my mentor. All I knew was I didn't have to stay at home.

In the first part of summer, I was hanging out at my friend Jake's house, who also attended Maytown. We started to get close toward the end of the school year. I wanted to hang with him because he was going to a different high school. He, Anthony, Lonny, and I hung out together. He lived within biking distance from our house, so I rode my sister's bike to get there. We played basketball on his court, played video games, or rode to the gas station to get snacks. That was the first time I tried tropical Sprite. I used to drink Sprite like it was going out of style.

The other thing we tried to get into was messing with girls. I was single at the time. Brooklyn was in her mode of playing games, so I cut that off. Jake was with his longtime girlfriend, and I was on the prowl like any hormonal fourteen-year-old. Jake knew a girl who lived by him and tried to hook us up. She was a pretty white girl named Heather. She was the same age as us.

She was home alone one day, and I went over there. I was nervous as heck. There wasn't a promise of anything about to go down, but the possibility of something made me nervous. We went into her room, and my nervousness got worse as I thought about her parents coming home and catching us. We began to kiss, and a thought crept across my mind regarding what I had heard about her reputation of "getting around." Of course, I didn't tell her this, but I said that I couldn't do it. She wondered why I was being a chump, and I just said I couldn't. I walked out, and she wasn't happy with me. When Jake asked me about it later, I told him that I couldn't get past her reputation, and he called me crazy. I ended up hanging out at his house periodically, until we both went to our respective high schools.

The summer was just as fun as I expected it to be, but somehow I got embroiled in more girl drama involving another girl whom I liked. My cousin Derrick and I, and some other friends from the neighborhood, were at the pool most of the day and into the night. At the pool, they had a sauna that was available for use, and we played around in there.

There was a white girl by the name of Chelsea, who didn't live in our neighborhood or the apartments but lived close. I was spitting game to her and feeling on her. By this time, I was a year or so removed from attending the Center, which taught me a lot about black history and caused me to feel uneasy about dating outside my race. I felt like it was something I shouldn't do because of our complicated history with white people. But over time, I became a little more comfortable with dating outside my race.

Meanwhile, in the background, Derrick liked her and was trying to get with her, but I didn't know this. He got word that I was spitting game to Chelsea and was upset about it. The funny thing about it was that he didn't even confront me; Drew's brother Maliq did. He was chubby, funny, and mostly always getting involved with the happenings in the neighborhood. He was two years older than me. He ended up confronting me about it, and we got into a heated exchange. I tried to tell him and my cousin that I didn't know he was trying to talk to her, and I was appalled I didn't know, considering we shared a room together.

As I continued to plead my innocence, Maliq wasn't having it and continued to antagonize me. I continued to get frustrated and called him out on his shenanigans. We squared up as if we were going to fight, and he put me in a headlock. He didn't punch me or anything, just a headlock. Derrick told us to break it up, and we went home.

The next day, Drew informed me that Maliq was talking smack throughout the neighborhood, saying that he beat me up. I immediately got pissed and wanted to exact revenge on that fat fool. I was at my cousin Kevin's house as usual that summer. Maliq came over with Drew and my cousins Derrick and Jacob. Maliq had caught wind of my challenge and accepted it. I let it be known that I wasn't cool with him talking smack behind my back and saying that he beat me up when that wasn't the case.

We were in the middle of the street in front of my cousin's house, and once again, he put me in a headlock. This time, I wasn't about to just take it, even though he was bigger than me. I knew I wasn't going to overpower him, so I just started punching him in his stomach and back as hard as I could until he let me go and got some cheap shots in before we were stopped by a guy who lived down the street, who threatened to call the police.

I went into my cousin's garage, and they went back toward our house. I wouldn't say I won the fight because it wasn't a fight that I was proud of or wanted to be a part of, but one thing was for sure: I wasn't about to back down to anyone. At this point in my life, I was still harboring a lot of anger and frustration from my past abuse and not having my mother in my life, so I was ripe and ready to attempt to beat down anyone who was trying to step to me for a challenge. I eventually mellowed out and didn't fight again until tenth grade.

Everything at the house was going as it normally went. My sister was up and down, intermittently getting along with Veronica. The thing that started to deteriorate in that home for me was Mr. Williams's drinking habit. We had no way of knowing he was a drinker during our first visit. I am certain that Mrs. Williams told him to be on his best behavior because she ran things in the house. This made me apprehensive and nervous about what he was capable of because he was a loud, obnoxious drunk, often being very confrontational. The first time I saw him get drunk and be confrontational, it made me think of the time when I was with Luther. Mr. Williams was a big guy like him, and it made me not want to be home when he was like that.

He and Mrs. Williams got into arguments about this often, and it didn't get better as the time went on. Austin and Mr. Williams got into a confrontation one day because Austin was not having it. He was frustrated with the problems in the home and was at his wits' end. I thought they would go to blows, but it never got to that point. He ended up moving out and getting his own place. That left a void in the home, and the Williamses were eager to fill up the spot in the house. Neither of the Williamses worked. They both took care of us by taking us to school, picking me up from practice, taking us to appointments and other duties.

One day my caseworker visited and asked me about how I felt about my eleven-year-old brother, Luther Jr., staying with us. You'd think I would have jumped at the idea of being reunited with my brother and to have the three of us living together, but that was not the case. I was apprehensive because of the journey my brother had experienced. When we split up again, my brother had experienced more abuse at the hands of his aunt, whom he lived with, and he eventually was sent to live at a group home owned and run by the same man who oversaw the Center. When my brother got to that group home, he was doing so well. I had not seen him like that before, and every time I saw him, he was in a good mood. He bragged about the allowance he would get and the help he was receiving.

The owner of the group home had a history of making waves with at-risk youth, and he had my brother Luther Jr. wrapped around his finger. My brother was in a good place, and I wasn't okay with taking him from an environment that was working so well for him. He had been through enough, and part of me wanted to protect him from further disappointment. When they questioned me about it, I explained to them that having him live with us would not be the greatest idea because we would be taking him out of a good environment, and we wouldn't be able to provide him with the resources that he had in the group home.

Mrs. Williams didn't buy it, and I believed she thought I was being selfish and wanted this family for myself and my sister. Against my very strong wishes, they decided to put the plan in motion. It was bittersweet. In one sense, I knew that I loved my brother and wanted him to be with my sister and me. In another sense, I knew that he was happy and doing well at the group home.

This was the second thing that they did that left a bitter taste in my mouth regarding their motives. I started to think, at that point, that they were in it for the money, not because they cared about the kids they were taking care of. This was disappointing because I was so sure that this would be the home for me, with a mom and dad and siblings who cared, and that was slowly turning into not being the case. I finally realized what Austin was trying to tell me from the beginning, and Operation Selfish Me was in full swing. I realized if I wanted to get to where I wanted to be in life, I needed to look out for myself first and then my siblings and no one else. I was only going to trust those who proved themselves trustworthy.

CHAPTER 20

Unresolved Issues

As the summer ended, I got more and more excited about high school. The prospect of being a ninth grader was scary, but I was excited nonetheless. It came time to get our schedules and take our class pictures. We had already gone school shopping using the money we made from working a job in a program that Derrick and I were part of. We went to the mall and got clothes and shoes that had me ready to dress to impress at school. I decided to wear this cut-off Rocawear shirt that I got from Burlington for the school ID picture.

I also signed up to play football, and practice was scheduled to begin before the start of school. It was hot that summer; I got darker from being in the sun so much. We didn't necessarily have a good football team at Wayman, but we played our hearts out and partied after the games.

School started, and I was taking pre-algebra, biology, English, physical education, and Spanish. Unfortunately, I had upperclassmen in my biology and pre-algebra classes, and that made it hard to focus and do well. I ended up getting Ds in both of those classes, and I was not happy about that. My other classes went well, including PE, which was a piece of cake. I could never understand why people didn't have an A in PE.

I also had my fair share of girl problems at the beginning of the year. I started talking to this black girl named Renee. I liked her, but I wasn't sure how my friends felt about her, so I didn't make it public that we were talking. We would write notes to each other, and that was something I looked forward to every day.

I was beginning to dislike football because the losses started to pile on, and once again, I wasn't asserting myself when it came to playing. I played like an all-star in my neighborhood, but I was just another player on the freshman team, playing cornerback and wide receiver. Toward the end of the season, one of our linemen suffered an injury, and it left a position open at the defensive line. Mind you, I was 5'4" and 140 pounds soaking wet as a freshman. I had no business being on the line, but I ended up getting a sack on the very first play.

I started the next game against a good team at home, which my mentor showed up to support. The Williamses never once attended my games. I understood. I wasn't their only kid. They also recently had a baby who took away any attention that was left.

As the school year progressed, my brother continued to be a handful. They were getting more and more fed up with his antics, and after only a few months into him staying there, they decided to move him out of the house. I had a bit of "I told you so" and anger because I knew that would happen, and he wasn't going to have the option of getting back into the group home. I was so frustrated because I tried to prevent it, and they tried to make it seem like it was because they wanted us to be together, but I thought it was for the money the whole time.

I started to grow more and more frustrated with staying there, and I tried to be away from the house as much as possible, staying the night at my cousin's or a friend's. I felt uncomfortable there; I felt like it was just a place for me to lay my head. It wasn't a home anymore; it was a place for bed, clothes, and food.

My friendship with Jason and Sean became that much more important. They both went to Maytown with me and were now at the same high school. Jason was white and Mexican, and Sean was black. Jason mostly lived with his dad, but he would visit his mom every other weekend. Whenever he was at his mom's, I tried to hang out with him or stay the night there because his mom lived in the apartments we frequented. It was a way to get away from the house, and we liked the same things. We played football and video games and went to the mall or movies.

His mom really became another mother figure for me because she saw me as a son once Jason and I formed our friendship. When I tried to be out of the house, there were a couple of times when I went over there even when I knew Jason wasn't. She joked around about it being weird, but what she didn't know was that I was trying to escape, not being comfortable in the home I was living in.

Jason and I also got into some trouble at times. One day we went to the store, and typically, his mom would give him money, and he would have enough for both of us, if I didn't have any. He did have money, but for whatever reason, this particular day, he just felt like taking something. Once I saw how it easy it was to take something, I participated as well. We had a good system that enabled us to evade the cameras, and then we would still buy something so it didn't seem like we stole anything. We participated in this scheme so many times that they ended up moving the camera from one aisle to the aisle we stole from. I was nervous at first, but we would get away with it so much that I started to become numb to it. This led to stealing from other places.

One time Jason, Sean, and I were at the local department store by Sean's house to get snacks and poker chips to play Texas Hold'em. The World Series of Poker was starting to be televised more, and we got really interested in it. Jason made me believe that he stole some chips, so I grabbed some too. As he walked through the doors, I thought that I was going to be okay, and I was; the alarm didn't go off. When we got out and were walking back to Sean's place, he told me he didn't steal any, and I was mad.

Another time, we were together at a different department store, and I saw that they had *The Boondocks* DVD for sale, and I had to have it. After I tore the packaging apart to get rid of anything that would set off the sensors, I put them in my pocket. As we approached the door, I was nervous as heck, and then the inevitable happened. The alarm went off. The lady at the door yelled for me to come back, and I kept going to the car.

Meanwhile, Sean and Jason were walking superslow as I motioned them to hurry up. Not only did they take their time but Sean also yelled to me, calling my name, to come back. I was so mad at them for that, but they failed to realize I wasn't ready to face the possible consequences. I was lucky she didn't chase after me, and since I didn't see any security around, I was trying to hurry up and get out of there before I got caught.

There was a situation that stopped me from stealing from stores again. I didn't consider myself a thief; I just made bad decisions. I didn't steal from family, friends, or any person for that matter, just from stores. Maybe that was how I convinced myself that it was okay all the time.

One day while going to the convenience store, this particular time, I went with Johnathon, who was a year younger than me and lived in the apartments across the street. I felt weird about the whole thing, so I opted to not steal anything. My intuition was right because the store owner had been trying to catch us; he'd had enough of our stealing from his store. He locked the doors and kept us in there. Unfortunately for him, he had other innocent customers whom he had to let out, and Johnathon took the opportunity to rush out when he did.

I was left there, but I was calm because I knew I didn't take anything this time. I'm not sure he had any proof that I took anything before then. As he interrogated me, he realized I didn't steal anything and wanted me to snitch on my friend. Of course, I wasn't going to snitch on him, and he finally let me go. As I walked back, I told myself I wasn't going to steal again.

My older cousin Matt was our barber. He came over and cut everyone's hair in the house. Jacob had braids, so he didn't get a cut, but he would get lineups every now and then. Matt got the pulse of how it was living there, and I didn't give it away too much. That didn't stop him from making the money they paid him to cut everyone's hair. He established such a good rapport that he was invited to come and cut every time we needed it.

I started to put my attention back to getting adopted. I was adamant that I wanted this before I moved into this place, and it wasn't going to change. I was really starting to get fed up because, now that I was older, they made me go to these mandatory weekend classes for life skills. It was learning how to iron, cook, balance a checkbook, manage finances, and do laundry, just to name some. Now that I look back, I realize they were helpful, but say that to a freshman in high school spending Saturday mornings at these classes. It sucked, and it made me want to be out of the system that much more.

The system dealt its final blow to the relationship I had with my mom. She finally terminated her rights, officially shutting the door to any chance we would have to live with her again until we turned eighteen. My dad was forced to give up his rights when he was in jail. I was never going to live with my dad, but the thought of never living with my mom again hit me tough. I didn't show it, though. I hid my feelings a lot around that time, and I let them out in sports. I was always so competitive, and I contribute that to unresolved issues.

The school year moved on, and I was still being made fun of because of the bags under my eyes and my big head, two things I had no control over. It wasn't as bad because being on the football team gave me more friends than foes. However, having bags under my eyes has always made me a target for jokes.

One person who really gave me a hard time was Mark. He was a well-off white kid who was a star in baseball, football, and basketball. We got along at times, but he mainly would piss me off because he would always talk crap about me. I threatened to beat him up a few times, but it never got to that point.

It is something that, to this day, has me looking in the mirror, wondering what it would be like if I didn't have bags under my eyes. Years and years of frustration and self-hate have had me contemplate that question often.

That fall, my mentor was looking out for me again. He suggested to one of the assistant principals at my school to take me and other students at my high school to a conference for young black males. It was the Indiana Commission on the Social Status of Black Males. It was a two-day event, and we dressed up and attended it. It was statewide, bringing leaders from across the state to Indianapolis to have a critical conversation about how to advance the black males in the community. They had dynamic speakers, and it was an awesome event to be part of. The keynote that year was Judge Mathis. He kept it real with us with his profound words. It was so awe-inspiring to be part of that event, and it influenced me in such a great way.

We attended a Colts game on one of the days, and it was my first professional football game to watch live. We didn't have great seats, but it was the thought that counted. It was fun to experience that, and I don't think I realized how blessed I was to have such great experiences.

I went to church every now and then but not like how it was when I was living with Granny. We didn't attend the same one, but we went to this predominantly white church that would pick us up in vans. I went with Derrick, and I was convinced that he only went because his girl went there, but I digress. I thought that I did some crazy things that I knew God wouldn't approve of, and I felt like it was a joke that I even went. Mr. Williams was a Jehovah's Witness so he attended those services every now and then, but he never made us join him. It was something he did on his time to get away from the house.

At school, basketball season was starting back up; and once again, I tried out to see if I could make it on the freshman team. I simply wasn't tall enough and didn't make it. I stayed in the weight room, bulking up for football, getting ready for the next sport to start.

One day when I was in a weight-room session, I put my fresh all-white midtop Air Force 1 shoes with the fat laces outside the room because I wasn't going to work out in them. When I came out after the session, they were gone. I was so devastated, and I tried to figure out who did it, to no avail. I knew that they were material things and that they didn't mean much, but after years of being picked on for having non-name-brand clothing and shoes, it was frustrating. And to have them stolen while I was working out really pissed me off. That was the time that Murphy Lee and the St. Lunatics came out with the song "Air Force Ones," and they were big at that time. I ended up going home that day with my workout shoes, and I didn't own another pair of Forces until my freshman year in college.

I didn't want to run track in high school, even though I ran in middle school. I thought it would be difficult to do, so I planned to chicken out and not run. Instead, I tried out for freshman baseball and didn't make the team. One day the track coach asked me if I had run before and told me to come out. I liked the idea that he wanted me to be on the team, and I said okay. He really liked that I already knew how to hurdle, so I would run those, even though most people were scared to. I solicited my mentor to get me the shoes I needed to run in, and he willingly hooked me up with gear. He also gave me pointers as he was a track athlete when he was in school.

Practices were hard, and it was difficult to keep up at first, but I adjusted. I was also a freshman, so I wasn't planning on breaking any records. One person who made a huge impact on the track team as a freshman was Drew, who in middle school was one of the fastest guys in the school. He ended up running track in middle school with his basketball shoes. I thought it was an amazing feat, but the dude was just multitalented. The most fun part of being on the track team was when we traveled to away track meets.

The first track meet that I went to was an indoor meet at Purdue University in West Lafayette. The track was small compared with the outdoor track; it was only two hundred meters. It looked like people were going so fast. It was definitely fun to be on a team that was fairly successful. We had some talented members on the track team. I ran in the junior varsity part of the meet. I didn't quite get hurdling yet, so I wasn't good enough to be on the varsity.

At season's end, every year, we hosted the sectional and regional. The varsity ended up winning the sectional championship, which I felt proud to be part of. I was there every step of the way to support them as they went on to the state meet. I became a fan, and I fell in love with the sport of track and field.

CHAPTER 21

On Track

The school year ended on a decent note, and my grades were mediocre. They weren't as great as I knew they could be, and I wanted to make sure I turned them around going into tenth grade. The summer was here, and I was off to my usual adventures. As I became more and more apathetic when it came to living in the home, I made it known that I had wanted to be adopted and that I was frustrated that it hadn't happened yet.

There had been conversations happening in the background among my granny and other family members. Kevin's mom, Aunt Q., was taking the necessary steps to bring me into her home to stay with her, my cousin Kevin, and his sister, Ashley. I was always over there, and it was one of my favorite spots to be in. I loved the idea. There was a chance I would finally get my wish of being adopted. I started the process by working on my caseworker, which would take some time.

The summer was another eventful one, helping my mentor with the golf tournament, taking a trip to Indianapolis for the Black Expo, and swimming in the pool in the apartments. There was one thing that was different about this summer. I started talking to Nicole, who was the younger daughter of Luther's ex-girlfriend, whom he took from his friend who passed away. I tried to get at her when I was younger, but she wasn't having it. My persistence paid off because she finally stopped playing games and took me seriously.

That summer, I visited her house quite a bit, and we hung out. One time she invited me over, and her mom wasn't home, and we were about to have sex. She asked me if I had ever done it, and I bragged that I did when I was in second grade. It seemed outrageous to her, so she grilled me on it. I explained to her that I humped on a girl while naked, and she told me that I didn't have sex. I was embarrassed because I had gone a long time thinking I was not a virgin, and she burst my bubble.

As I realized I was a virgin, we attempted to rid me of that moniker, but we were so nervous that it didn't go right. She was a virgin at the time as well, and we both stayed that way because I ended up leaving the house before anything happened. We continued to talk, not really making it official but staying good friends.

That summer didn't have much drama because I wasn't too concerned with pleasing anyone or doing anything that would get me in trouble. I was in get-out-of-this-house mode. Mr. and Mrs. Williams continued to provide for me and do what I deemed the essentials: feed me, clothe me, and bring me to my appointments. I started visiting the allergy doctor to check on my allergies and asthma. I even considered getting my bags taken away because I have long been told that my bags were due to allergies.

They also brought me to football practice that summer, and I continued to improve. I was starting to gain confidence and the attention of the coaches as we trained to get ready for the season. During a drill, I was head-to-head with the starting corner for the varsity, and we were struggling to take each other down. I got tired of wrestling and let up for a second, and the other guy slammed me to the ground. As I tried to get up from my fall, I felt a pain hit my left wrist like no other. The trainer checked it out, and it didn't look good. She gave me ice and told me to get to the hospital as soon as possible. I wasn't sure what was wrong, but I knew it hurt like heck.

We got to the hospital, and the doctor took an X-ray. I had dislocated my left wrist at the radial bone. The doctor decided that he wasn't going to do surgery on it. His plan was to pop it back in place. He didn't numb me or put me to sleep. He had one of the nurses hold my hand, and then he popped it back in place. Of course, I screamed like a baby because it hurt; but afterward, I was ready to get a cast on. He gave me instructions on how to take care of my cast and set me up with a follow-up doctor to help me recover.

It happened so fast that I didn't get a chance to take in everything until I was at home with my cast, lying in bed. I was scheduled to be out of football for at least six weeks. I wasn't getting my cast off until four weeks after the injury happened. When school started, I got some attention because people wanted to know what happened to my arm. Too bad it wasn't on my writing arm. I would not have been able to write and wouldn't have had to do assignments, at least not on my own.

Despite everything I was going through at that time, I made a commitment to have better grades that school year. I got off to a much better start than I did the previous year. I came in with a different focus. I was less concerned with who people thought I was trying to be or not to be. I needed to get on track and stay there.

I started the school year at the Williamses' home, but I didn't stay there. I had put a bug in my caseworker's ear that I wanted to be adopted and that I had someone in mind. She did her due diligence, and my aunt Q. was ready to take me in. As Aunt Q. was preparing for that to happen, she got this idea of softening the blow on the Williamses. To this day, I am not sure what her motives were, but it was a day that could've messed the Operation Adoption all up.

One day I was at Aunt Q.'s house, and the Williamses wanted me to come home. Mr. Williams came to pick me up, and everything was supposed to be routine. Somehow Aunt Q. got to Mr. Williams's weakness of drinking, and next thing you know, he was drunk. He had come over to pick me up and wasn't able to bring me home after that, so I was waiting to see what would happen next. Mrs. Williams came, and she wasn't happy with Mr. Williams or my aunt. That was the beginning of some bad blood between the two, and I thought things were going to take a turn for the worse.

My caseworker had finally met with me and the Williams family and asked questions about who I was trying to move with. When asked about my prospective adoptive parent, Mrs. Williams told my caseworker that she didn't have anything to say about her because of the bad taste she left in her mouth. The caseworker also asked me if I wanted my sister to come, and Mrs. Williams blurted out, "No, he is only thinking about himself." I interjected by stating the fact that my goal all along was to be adopted and that it was supposed to be set in motion when I moved there. Instead, I was told that I was "too old" to be adopted and that they wouldn't do it. I wanted to fulfill this wish for the reason of not having to be a part of the system.

Even though they were not down to adopt me, they had agreed to adopt my sister. I didn't like living there, but my sister seemed to really enjoy it most of the time. I was fine with leaving her with the Williamses because they could take care of her and maybe love her. I felt I had to do what was best for me, so I left. I was set to move with Aunt Q. and my cousins, Kevin and Ashley, after football season.

I was still recovering from the injury. They did X-rays to check on it, and they even put a new color on my cast. When it was time to take the cast off, my arm was smelly and small. It was so weird. However, I was so happy to have it off. They ended up giving me a soft cast, and I was so excited to wash my arm and get back to work, to play with my teammates. I went to physical therapy the next couple of weeks, and I finally got cleared to return to practice and games.

In my first game back, I earned a spot on the kickoff return team, returning kicks for the junior varsity team. I wasn't on the front line; I was going to run the ball. This was new because I had not blossomed into the player I was capable of being, and it was an opportunity to prove myself. I was also scheduled to start at wide receiver and maybe even play a little running back.

I got the first kickoff, and I don't remember much after that. I believe I had a concussion, but the athletic trainer didn't think so. I still don't remember anything after that point in the game, and I don't remember the score. I don't even remember how I got home that night. I just remember waking up in my bed at home; looking at my wrist, which was taped for the game; and trying to figure out what day it was. I truly didn't know, and it made me wonder if I was misdiagnosed that night. It is part of my memory that I just don't recall.

The season ended as quickly as it started. I was ready to move with Aunt Q. I said my goodbyes to the Williams family and a special goodbye to my little sister. I truly had intentions to be adopted; that was all I ever wanted. I didn't want to get on anyone's bad side or upset or abandon my little sister. This family was not willing to adopt me because of my age, and I didn't think that was fair, considering that I had wanted that all along. I was made out to look like the selfish person, and in all honesty, I think I realized that no one was going to take care of me better than I was. I had to look out for my best interests no matter what because people were going to look out for their own best interests. At that point, I was going to appreciate what was done for me, but I wasn't about to let my guard down too much to avoid being disappointed or hurt in that way again.

CHAPTER 22

Milestones

I wasn't adopted right away as the process had to take its course. When I moved in with Aunt Q., I was technically still in foster care. Nonetheless, I loved everything about living with her. I shared a room with my cousin Kevin. I had always admired this home, and now I was living there. It was something that I thought was awesome, and I thought I was finally going to be happy and appreciated.

Every little detail about staying there stood out for me. I used an electric toothbrush for the first time, my breath was fresh with the Aquafresh toothpaste, and I even rode the bus to school on a different route. I was really starting to settle in there. My cousins and aunt really helped make me feel comfortable.

There would be times when I would get into it with Kevin and Ashley, but that was your typical brother-and-sister banter because they became like siblings for me. We fought and argued in the home, but when we got to school, we had one another's backs. I kept in touch with Derrick and Jacob because I still saw them in school, and I didn't live far from there. I also wanted to check on my sister periodically, just to see how she was doing. I was always trying to make sure that I didn't make a mistake by leaving her at that home.

At my new home, my obsession for pornography reached an all-time high. My cousin Kevin had downloaded these pornos on the desktop computer, and I watched them when no one was home or late at night when everyone was asleep. We even watched them together at times, but most of the time, I watched them alone. I didn't really share this obsession with anyone because I thought that people would think that I was weird, but it was a real problem I had, which only made my masturbation addiction worse. There were times when I just had to do it no matter what.

At school, it was as if I had never moved. My counselor called me into the office to see if I would be interested in applying to a program called Telluride Association Sophomore Seminar (TASS). They had two sessions going on at Indiana University Bloomington and the University of Michigan in Ann Arbor. The process to apply was stringent, and you had to write essays along with your application. If you were selected for the program, you spent six weeks on a college campus, staying in the dorms, eating in the dining halls, and taking a class Monday through Friday. It sounded like a great thing to me, so I committed to applying.

I enlisted help from my English teacher, Mrs. Greene, who was my favorite teacher at the time. She was my favorite because she was nice, but she was also good-looking for her age. It made it difficult, at times, to focus in her class. I wrote the essays, and I didn't do so well on them. At the time, I wasn't the best writer. She really helped me formulate what I was trying to say and assisted me in turning in some solid essays. I felt confident that I did well on the application and was anxious to hear back.

I wanted Nicole, the girl whom I had been talking to periodically, to come over and check out my new spot. She finally got her mom to bring her over one night, and I was so excited. When she arrived, we started watching television, and I had no intentions to do anything with her beyond that. Then we started to talk and cuddle, and I asked her if she would be down to do something. She was hesitant because my aunt and cousins were home. I assured her that I would make sure my cousins would stay upstairs and let me know if Aunt Q. came out of her room. I sweet-talked her, and she was good to go.

I went upstairs to get a rubber, and we had sex. It happened so fast that she asked me, "Already?" I told her I didn't want to get caught, but she wasn't satisfied. As I went in the restroom to clean up, I wondered to myself why I hadn't felt anything like that before. It was probably a good thing that I didn't know how to have sex until then because I could've been subjected to teenage pregnancy. We continued to watch a movie until it was time for her to go, and we agreed to keep talking.

The next day at school, I bragged to some of my friends that I lost my virginity, and they laughed at me because of how quick it was. It was my first time. What did they expect? I didn't know what I was doing. All I know was that I hadn't felt anything like that, and it was a great feeling.

I mentioned before that my aunt had worked at this big company for many years. Shortly before I moved in, she decided to retire from her job and open her own nonprofit, helping battered women. I am not sure what truly happened, but all I know is that it didn't work out for her. That really weighed on her tough. I saw how things affected her, and her drinking became troublesome over time. She also took a hit financially. My cousins weren't getting the nice things or ample food that they were accustomed to, and my moving in didn't help. It made for a tough Christmas that year, and she informed us that we wouldn't get many, if any, presents that year.

I felt I was partly to blame at times because, when I moved in, I believed I added to her burdens. My cousins did everything but blame me directly for the struggles. I was already in defense mode, looking out for myself every chance I got, because I was tired of moving around, and I was frustrated with being disappointed. That attitude and shift in my thinking from my prior home led to my butting heads with Aunt Q.

My mentor would often give me things for my birthday or for Christmas, and that year, it wasn't any different. He gave me $100, and I went to the mall and bought myself a pair of shoes. At that time, they had this deal at most shoe stores where you could get two pairs of shoes for $89.99. I purchased the deal, and I got them gift-wrapped at this free wrapping booth just because I could. I brought them home and put them under the tree. It was the only thing under the tree at the time, until my aunt could get a couple more.

On Christmas Day, we opened the little presents that were there, and I pretended to be surprised about the new shoes. That rubbed my cousins and aunt the wrong way. She didn't appreciate the fact I was being selfish and only got things for myself, knowing that this would be a tough Christmas. I felt bad because my intent wasn't to hurt anyone. I just wanted to make sure I was happy, but I saw how that could be selfish at times. I decided to take the shoes back. I ended up getting something for my aunt and cousins, and I felt better about that.

The New Year began, and I finally heard back from TASS. I was selected to take the next step, which was an interview. My interview was with a Telluride volunteer who was an alumnus of the program, and they helped determine if I too would be chosen to participate in it. I let Aunt Q. know where the interview would be, and she agreed to bring me there. This program was free; the only thing you paid for was travel.

The demand to be in this program was at an all-time high. As I went to the interview, I was nervous. I didn't know what to expect or even what to say. Aunt Q. gave me good advice, and I went with it. After the interview, I felt good. They informed me that I wouldn't hear back for several weeks, and the wait was on.

Track season was on us, and I was ready to have a better season than my freshman year. Football didn't go as expected because of my injury, and I wanted to redeem myself, if I could. I started the off-season working hard to get ready for the season. I continued to improve in school with more solid grades. I was down to just about one person making fun of me regularly. He was the same kid from freshman year. I also got a couple of behavior referrals here and there but nothing major, except for the time I got suspended for fighting.

By the time I got to high school, I mellowed out when it came to my anger. A lot of the things that were causing my anger were starting to be nonexistent in my life. Aside from the fights I had in eighth grade and outside school, I kept the peace for the most part. I was now sixteen years old, and it took a lot for me to get angry enough to fight people at this point in my life. It was a surprise to most when I finally got into a fight in class.

We were in the first period, watching the daily news run by our school. Not paying attention, I decided to have a conversation with Sean, who was in my class and sat behind me. To speak with him, I rested my elbow on the kid's desk behind me. Well, he must've been having a bad day because he didn't like that and told me to get my damn elbow off his desk. I thought that was a little extreme and didn't feel like it was necessary, but I wasn't going to make anyone feel uncomfortable. As I turned back around to face the front of the classroom, he continued to talk smack about me.

Now at this point, everyone around us could hear what was going on. It didn't help that there were upperclassmen in the class. One of them started to aggravate the situation, and I was close to losing my cool. As the commotion got louder, I decided that I couldn't take any more of his crap. I stood up in front of his desk—fists clenched, frustrated, and angry—and yelled, "Shut the f—— up talking to me like that before I beat you down!" He stood up, feeling threatened, and I thought at that point that things would escalate further. When he stood up, I turned away as if I were going to walk away, and then I saw red. I cocked back and punched him as hard as I could in the face, and the boxing match ensued.

I was swinging as fast and as hard as I could. Somehow we ended up on the floor, and I was on top of him, pounding his face with my fist. Finally, someone broke it up; and at that point, I didn't know if I won or not, so I didn't celebrate right away. I saw that his nose was bloody, and I knew I had gotten the best of him. I started talking smack at that point, and then the march to the principal's office was on. I was walking with pride that I won the fight. He was walking in defeat with a bloody nose.

As we entered the office, he went to the nurse to clean up, and I was in the assistant principal's office, who was a black man. Once the other kid got cleaned up, we both were sitting in his office. He asked why we did it, and we told him that it was stupid. We both barely got into trouble and had never been suspended before this fight. We both got two days' suspension, and that was that.

I caught up with my friends later, and they let me know that it got around that I won the fight, but of course, they had to add to it. They made fun of me because I beat up a gay guy. The kid wasn't out, but it was something we all suspected. I think he struggled with that throughout high school, but we didn't give him a hard time for it. Instead of giving me props for beating the guy up, they gave me a hard time for beating up a gay guy. I couldn't win. That was the last time I got into a fight. I just committed myself to not fight anymore unless I absolutely had to. People didn't try to press me that much, so I was good to go.

I finally got the letter in the mail from TASS. I was so anxious to open it that I tore it open. As I read the letter, my mood changed from excitement to disappointment. I was an alternate. I didn't believe anyone would turn down the opportunity to do this, not thinking about other reasons why a person might give up their spot, such as illness or some other emergency, so I didn't think there was a chance I could go, and I wrote it off. Life went on.

Track had started, and I was traveling with the team to the various track meets. We traveled a lot to different indoor and outdoor meets, and I had a blast. I was doing better and competing more that season since I had gotten a little faster and could compete. I still wasn't the fastest on the team, but I wasn't the slowest either. We still had some talented people on the track team, and I tried to be at every meet.

A few weeks later, I received an e-mail from TASS, and I was surprised. I was offered a spot in the TASS program, and I gladly accepted. I jumped up and down with excitement and told Aunt Q. I was going to spend my whole summer at IU. I completed tenth grade, and it was probably my strongest year academically in all my high school years.

The summer started off great, and I anticipated going to the program. I was getting things ready to go. It was scheduled to start the last week of June and go until the first week of August. My aunt decided that she wasn't going to bring me there, so my mentor volunteered, but he wasn't going to be able to pick me up because he would be out of town. That would be an issue later. I was excited to experience something new and get away from Fort Wayne. I really took every opportunity to get away from the city. It was wearing on me, and I was ready for something new. I had aspirations to go to college outside Fort Wayne as I was a 21st Century Scholar, who would get their tuition taken care of for any school in the state of Indiana.

As I said goodbye to my aunt and cousins, Mr. Hayes and I hit the road to Bloomington. As the cornfields kept going by and we passed the cars in the slow lane, I thought about the journey I was getting ready to take. I thought about what the other students would be like. Would they be boring? Would they be really smart? Would they be mean, like the people I had interacted with before? Would they accept me for who I was or at least trying to be? So many questions and so many thoughts were swirling through my mind.

We stopped at Cracker Barrel before we continued our journey. That place had really good country food. They had breakfast, lunch, and dinner; and all of it was good, especially their fried catfish. We ate and were back on the road again. An hour or two passed before we arrived in Bloomington.

CHAPTER 23

Real World Bloomington

The beautiful campus that I have come to know and love all these years was going to be my home for the longest amount of time yet. We pulled up to the Mason Hall dorm. Mason Hall dorms were used as apartments during the school year, and we were using the building for the next six weeks. We were all sixteen or seventeen years old, going into eleventh grade. The girls stayed on one side and the boys on the other. When I arrived, there were already folks moving and helping people get their things together. Dillon offered to help me bring my stuff in, and Mr. Hayes, being the generous person that he was, gave him some cash for his troubles. Once I was settled in, I hugged and thanked Mr. Hayes, and he made his way back to Fort Wayne.

I went up the stairs to be greeted by my roommate, Jackson, who was from the Bronx. He was superchill and down-to-earth, and I knew that we were going to get along. The room we shared was big, and we had plenty of room to spread our wings. The other guys in our suite had also arrived to the hall. Jerrell and Dillon shared a room. They both were from Illinois. Adam and Blake shared the last room in our three-bedroom suite. Adam was from Ohio, and Blake was from Indiana, like me. We were the only homers as everyone else was from out of state. Our suite also included a living room, a shared bathroom, and a kitchenette. I got along with all the boys, and we forged a bond that would only get stronger as time passed in the TASS summer program.

There were twelve girls who were there, and they all had different personalities. They were from about five different states. Being a single upcoming high school junior, I was thinking of who I would try to flirt with as time went on. They all were attractive in different ways, but there were a couple of girls who really caught my eye. As we all arrived and settled into our rooms, we got ready for our first official event together—dinner in our other home, the Wright Dining Hall. We ate all our meals in that hall, and that was the first of many.

This was also our first time getting to know one another a little more. People's personalities started to show, and I knew who I would ultimately gravitate to when forging friendships. We also had to prepare for the next day, which was the first day of class. Each day, we attended a three-hour seminar. It included discussions, small-group work, lectures by faculty, and other activities. We were expected to prepare for class and write several papers during the summer. Our tutors, as they were aptly named, Jalen and Christina, helped us polish up our writing skills as we progressed throughout the summer.

The theme was Films of the African American Experience: An Introduction to Film Studies. Our instructors were Indiana University professors—Professor Mack, a black woman, and Professor Wilson, a white woman. When we attended the session on the first day, we were surprised to find that Professor Wilson was white, and we joked about doubting that she could teach us about our history. All of us were minorities, most of us black. Professor Wilson proved herself very knowledgeable and capable of teaching about this subject.

I knew of my history because of how much I learned going to the Center on Saturday mornings and participating in events, but it had been some years since we attended the Center since moving from Granny's house. In TASS, I learned a lot more. This experience not only helped me from an educational standpoint but also made me learn so much from the other people who attended with me. We were some of the brightest minorities in the country, and we were all gathered at this place to learn, prepare for college, and forge bonds that could last a lifetime.

We watched and learned about some things that really had me reeling. When I learned about how they negatively portrayed black folk in movies, commercials, games, and television shows, I couldn't believe it. I was fuming. We learned about stereotypes, including Uncle Tom, mammy, Sambo, big lips, brutes, monkeys, mulattoes, and more. It was such a shock. I looked at things so differently. It made for great conversations and class discussions.

The first week went by quickly. We got into a routine of going to class, having lunch, exploring the campus, getting work done, and hanging out. I wasn't as strong of a writer as others in the program, and at times, I felt that I didn't belong because they all were so intelligent. I tried my best to keep up with them, but I got exposed during the first assignment. I had to meet with Jalen to go over the first paper, and he picked my paper apart. He knew I was capable of more, and I think he realized I hadn't been challenged until that point. He challenged me to work on it further, and this process helped me improve as a writer because he believed in me.

As for getting along with the people, six weeks was a long time living with strangers. We had our fair share of disagreements in the house. The main cause of most of the drama in the house was Blake. At the time, he was struggling with his own things, and that came to pass often. We got into a disagreement one time, and I literally had to leave the house because I was ready to fight him. That would have disqualified me, and I would have been sent home.

We watched all types of films that really challenged us to analyze everything. This experience was supposed to get us out of our comfort zone and really help us grow over the course of the summer. We were not allowed to bring a television, and there was only one television in the lounge, in the basement area, and we rarely turned it on—only for big television events or for movie night. We mostly had the pleasure of entertaining one another or going out and exploring the campus.

We would watch films in class from different eras, and we could see the evolution of black folks throughout. We also learned about well-known black actors and actresses of the times who paved a way for the folks who are on the screen today. The list of movies was endless, but some that come to mind were *Birth of a Nation, Super Fly, Coffy, Malcolm X, Bamboozled, Hollywood Shuffle, Boyz N the Hood, Do the Right Thing, Cooley High,* and *Ethnic Notions. Ethnic Notions* really messed me up. I knew about slavery, and I knew how brutal it was for my people, but if there was any doubt left in me about the struggle of my people, it was quickly gone after watching the documentary. It was a riveting film about stereotypes of black folk that were prevalent all throughout the history of postslavery. These stereotypes existed in cartoons, movies, songs, shows, and advertisements. If someone came to our country and didn't know its history, you would think we were lazy, ungrateful black folk who ate watermelon and sang songs about what it was like on the plantation.

Talk about being pissed off. I was fuming after watching this documentary, and after it went off, I made a vow to look at things differently. We were on edge. In my mind, I dared a white person to look at me wrong. These stereotypes have since subsided, but the aftereffect of it is still present in modern-day media, music, and television. This film was a coming-out party of sorts for me—to appreciate my blackness and embrace who I truly was. I pledged to no longer feel ashamed that I was black, and I wanted to make it a point to ensure that I knew who I was and what I was capable of. That documentary was one of the many things that truly helped me transform over the course of the summer.

Another important part of being in the TASS program was the friendships that I developed. I was really cool with my roommate and happy that they paired the people the way that they did. I also developed a bond with Jerrell from Chicago. This dude's taste in music was on par with mine, if not better. His wittiness and mild temperament made me want to hang with him, and another plus was that he played basketball. Besides my roommate, Jerrell was another person I knew I could definitely be friends with after we ended the program.

I formed another bond with Lauren. She was from Virginia, and I loved her personality from the beginning. The first time we got a chance to chat it up and get to know each other, I felt like I could talk to her for hours. There was something about being in the presence of someone so pretty and so smart that really made me attracted to her. I also loved how she accepted me for who I was—bags under my eyes and all. I didn't meet too many girls like that back at home. She was a powerful combination of smarts and looks, and I wanted to be more than friends with her, if possible. She didn't want to form anything more than a friendship because we would end up going our separate ways and having a long-distance relationship. We were tested as time went on to try to stay platonic, but that strong attraction made it tough.

To pass the time, some of the TASS participants and I often participated in random activities. Whether they were our epic basketball games or the random dances that we hosted, we had to do things that passed the time. It was summer on a primarily empty campus, and we had a lot of time to kill, outside of when we had work to do for class. When we got tired of eating dorm food, we decided to hit up an inexpensive restaurant with our spending money.

One time we were walking around and found a KKK symbol spray-painted on a wall. It scared the crap out of us because none of us had ever experienced anything like that. We were also on edge because of all the things we were learning in class about our history and how we fit into the present day. We were all rattled from that event, and we ended up bonding more. We were already learning some amazing things, but to experience that firsthand and to have that feeling was surreal.

We were about two weeks in when the Fourth of July holiday arrived. We were given the day off from class, and we tried to figure out how we would celebrate the occasion. We decided that we would barbecue. People volunteered to do certain things, and we made the most of it. It wasn't the best-tasting food, but they tried with what we had. We weren't exactly working with a deluxe kitchen. These strangers from across the country whom I met were starting to become more like family to me, and the more time that went by, the more I tried not to think about having to leave.

I ended up forming a great relationship with both of our tutors but more specifically with Jalen. We both were Indiana natives, but we connected on a level that was different from the other students in the program. I think he picked up on my not being as talented as the others were academically, and he wanted so badly for me to reach my potential. He saw in me what so many others were starting to see, and he really challenged me to do and be my best. That type of support was invaluable, and I continue to appreciate him for that.

Lauren and I continued to dance around the fact that we liked each other. We both knew and had heard about not getting connected on this level because of the inevitability that we would part ways and possibly not see each other again. The connection, and the fact that she was different from any girl I had ever connected with, made it impossible for me not to want to be with her, but we continued to be friends, which was tough. She would purposely try to distance herself from me because she could feel herself really connecting with me, and that frustrated me. I would do what my high school self would do: play games like I wasn't upset.

It was a crazy game of love, and eventually, love won. After the back-and-forth, we slightly became more than friends. The others knew how much we liked each other, and the countdown to the last day was on. All I wanted to do was cherish the last moments with the girl who had my heart.

The Black Expo was on us, and our tutors informed us that we would be taking a short trip up North to Indianapolis or Naptown. We were as excited as the *Big Brother* contestants when something interesting happened in the house. I always said the TASS experience was like being on the *Real World*. We jumped at the idea of doing something fun, so we all got ready like we were going to the hottest event in the world. Blake and I tried to let everyone know about how great it was and get them ready for another fun adventure, but it was something that they had to experience for themselves. It was another fun year, but it was different because I was going with my amazing peers. We had a blast and went back to Bloomington ready to tackle the rest of the weeks.

We were coming down to the wire, and we were all preparing for the last couple of days. We had an assignment to work on for the end-of-the-summer project, and we were all busy doing our usual things on top of preparing for this assignment. I ended up working with Dillon, Jerrell, and my roommate, Jackson. We decided that our project would be to rap about what we were learning. I decided to rap off the "Through the Wire" instrumental because Kanye West was my favorite rapper at the time, and Jerrell rapped to an old-school hip-hop beat. We worked on that thing until it was perfect. We ended up knocking that project out of the park. Everyone else had great presentations, and it just solidified my idea of being surrounded by so many talented people. It was such a blessing.

A day or two before we all went our separate ways, the professors invited us to their home to have a last hurrah with food and memories. We took a lot of photos, and the fact that we might never see one another again really started to set in. It was tough to think about. The day before was the toughest. I was already sad about what was about to happen, and my aunt Q. couldn't figure out who was going to pick me up because she originally didn't want to, but my mentor was out of town and couldn't. She finally decided to come, along with my cousins.

I also wondered what would happen with me and Lauren. Everyone warned us about getting emotionally involved, and that didn't stop us, and now we were about to be emotional wrecks. The night before, we just tried to console and tell each other we would meet again and that we would keep in touch, but that didn't make it easier.

The day of departure came, and it was one of the saddest days of my life. The enormity of the moment and the experience, learning what we did with the people I met and formed bonds with, could not have been better. To finally meet a girl who liked me for who I was, and I didn't have to be anything but myself, was huge for me. It was something I wasn't used to, and I was about to go home to a place that would not have a girl even remotely close to Lauren. The thought of that saddened me.

Lauren was scheduled to leave before me, and I gave her a hug, and she began to cry. The van drove away, and my heart began to ache. Someone forgot something, and five minutes later, they came back. She took the opportunity to say she wanted to try to make it work, even though we were states apart. I didn't care. At that point, I was in love and didn't think I would find another girl like that. We exchanged I-love-yous, and then she was officially on her way. All I had to remember her by, for the moment, were her bracelet and a letter she wrote me. We were officially boyfriend and girlfriend, and I was content.

Everyone else left one by one and some in groups for those who had to fly. Jerrell left with his beautiful family, and we hugged it out and wished each other the best. Jackson left, and I did the same for him. Then it was my turn. Aunt Q. showed up. I packed my things into the car, said goodbye to the people who were left, and began the long journey to Fort Wayne. I was left with my thoughts, wondering how I would move on with my life after this amazing experience and how to make a long-distance relationship work. It was tough to think about or fathom, but I was willing to try.

As we drove off and we were on the freeway, I broke down crying because I instantly missed my friends who used to be strangers but became much more than that. My cousin didn't understand, and I wasn't about to explain it to him. This was a moment to myself, and I needed it. I regrouped, and Operation Life after TASS was in motion.

CHAPTER 24

Goals

Football season was on us, and I was already behind in training. It was my junior year, and if I was ever going to have a coming-out party, this would be the year to do it. I was behind the curve, and we had a new coach, which meant a new system to learn. I was keeping in touch with Jason, who was also on the football team, while I was in Bloomington, and I worked out so I wouldn't be in terrible shape when I returned to the field. He tried to scare me into expecting the worst when I came back, but it wasn't all that bad. Practice was practice, and I was just trying to get back in the thick of things. I had this newfound confidence after such an awe-inspiring experience, and I wanted to make an impact on the team. I wore Lauren's bracelet so that I could have extra motivation and be reminded of our relationship.

The first scrimmage came, and we were away. I didn't get to start that time, so I waited until I got an opportunity, and when it came, I took advantage of it. I got into the game at cornerback and impressed coaches by making back-to-back impact plays. I also played as wide receiver and was close to scoring a touchdown on a big play, but the ball was just out of reach. Coach was impressed with my effort, and I think he found it refreshing to see someone play 100 percent. I ended up getting the starting corner position on the varsity team.

I was really feeling good at this point. Things were on the up and up. I had my girlfriend, school was about to start, and I was about to play varsity football. How could things get any better?

I didn't call home too often when I was away at Indiana University because I didn't necessarily want to. It was good to be away from my hometown, which I despised at times, even after high school. It was a place that I saw as negative, and the negative outweighed the positive.

Shortly after I was named the starting cornerback, set to start the game on Friday, Aunt Q. informed us that we were going to move to Indianapolis. I felt I had jinxed it. Things were going so well, and I was just starting to get my bearings, and now I was moving to another city and attending another school—my ninth school since kindergarten. It was bittersweet, and I didn't know what else to do but be excited that I would be going to a city that I always loved. We also found out that we would be attending the athletic juggernaut Whitney East. I was nervous and anxious, but it was another move that I had no control over, and I was at the mercy of my aunt. At least this time we were leaving the city I didn't like. As I said my goodbyes, I got more comfortable with moving to Nap as the days continued to count down. We were on our way, and I was excited about it. New beginnings, new adventures.

My relationship with Lauren, as we expected, could not stand the test of the long distance that plagued us, and the fact that we were young didn't help. We were in different parts of the country dealing with our own things, and it made it tough to commit to each other. We decided to break it off and be friends, but that didn't make it easy to accept. We went back and forth, ignoring each other and talking to each other. It really put a strain on the relationship we built, and it made it hard to be friends for a while. She was the first girl to really understand and accept me. I was on the market again, and I was in a mode where I was going to try to find any girl who could help me not think about Lauren. That was tough, though, and I hurt some girls in the process.

Indianapolis was as vibrant and poppin' as ever. We frequented this great city often, and we were familiar with the part of town that we were going to stay in: the east side of Nap, in the Whitney Township school district. We were a couple of days away from starting school as we registered for our classes, and my cousin Kevin and I were in awe of how big and immaculate the school was. The football stadium was huge. The school building was beyond huge, and it was in a nice neighborhood. My cousin Ashley stayed back home because she wanted to finish her senior year in Fort Wayne, so it was just Kevin and me until she finished up. Until then, she would stay with us on holidays and special occasions.

We stayed with my cousin Kenya, who was the mother of my cousin Daniel, who was the same age as Kevin. She had an apartment that was cozy, but she had room to fit us until my aunt got established and we could get our own place. We were in Nap for about two weeks before Aunt Q. got a job at Verizon Wireless, and then a couple of weeks later, we got a townhouse around the corner from Kenya's house and the school. Kenya lived right across the street from the school, so we would walk to and from there. Whitney East was everything we expected it to be. It was big, and it was diverse.

I immediately gravitated to the athletes because of my track background, and I was lucky enough to have one of the fastest guys in the state in my honors English class. After my stellar tenth-grade year and my summer TASS experience, I was challenging myself with a couple of tough classes. I held my own, but the adjustment from one school to the other was hard, and my grades suffered because of it. I didn't fail, but I wasn't getting all As and Bs like I did the year prior. Since I just earned a starting position on my old football team, I thought I would approach the football coach and ask if I could be on the team since I played at my last school. He said that they had enough players at my position and that I would be behind the curve, considering the season was in full swing. Instead, I signed up for off-season track so I could get ready for the season.

The first girl I tried to pursue post-Lauren was a twin. I was just trying to see what I could get with my charm, and I didn't get too far. The next girl was sweet, and I thought she was pretty. I was really trying to get past Lauren, and I was struggling miserably. I ended up breaking it off with her and getting with another girl, but that also didn't go well. She ended up breaking up with me during school in a letter. I was appalled because it wasn't like she was Halle Berry. I started to think that I wasn't going to find another girl who would like me for who I truly was.

At school, I had one close friend who just so happened to be new to the school as well. His name was Tyson, and he was from New Jersey. He was in the same grade as me. I really got to know him well, and then one day his dad brought us to a fair. Another kid in our grade, Brandon from Florida, joined us, and we became good friends as well. There we were, three friends, all from different states and cities, in the same place. They made the transition easier to deal with, and it was getting easier to keep my mind off the past.

At home, I was going through the motions. I hung out with Kevin or did my own thing. My aunt usually worked during the day, so she would come home later, but we didn't talk as much as we used to. I started to see that she wasn't as happy as I was with moving there, and that became a problem. I didn't want to think about moving again, so I kept my mind off it. Our neighborhood was quiet and chill, and we had a couple of stores within walking distance. I made my friends in my grade, and Kevin made his. For the first time in a couple of years, I had my own room, but that didn't last. As soon as Kevin's sister finished school, she moved down and joined us, and I went back to sharing a room with Kevin. I was planning on relishing having my own room until she got there.

Back at school, I had started my off-season weight-training class and got to lift with the football team and other athletes. It was like a college weight room. I had never seen anything like it. The trainer was intense and literally ran the weight room like a college program. They had names on the board for those who could join a club by lifting a certain amount of weight. I ended up getting on the 235-Pound Power Clean Club when I finally reached that goal. I got so strong over the next couple of months that I didn't know what to do with myself. I was in such great shape. I was literally having the time of my life at that school, and it hadn't even been a full year yet.

The other thing I loved about that school was the awesome breakfast and lunch. Lunch was à la carte style, so each day you could choose what you wanted to eat. Whether it was pizza or a special or if you wanted a wrap, it was your choice, and I loved it. Sometimes I would get my lunch and then steal Fruitopias or cookies because my new friends would do it. I always said that I would stop stealing after I got caught in the past, but I believed I had to have these things even though I didn't have the money to buy them.

I struggled in two classes: Spanish and chemistry. I took Spanish two years in a row, but this class was different. It just so happened that a black lady taught the class too. I struggled because she challenged us to really know it, and I could not grasp it. This was after my stellar sophomore year. I was on a high, and this brought me back down to the earth. In chemistry, the challenge to know more about the different symbols made it tough, and I was having a hard time with it. In that class, I made friends with a kid whose parents owned a costume factory. I noticed he would come in with wads of money, and I wanted to know how I could get some. I literally begged him to let me work with him, but he wasn't having it.

Football season ended with a state championship. That was one of the best teams I've ever witnessed. The team was full of D1-caliber players. Track season was on us, and we had begun doing preseason workouts. The school had an indoor track, so we could do workouts and hurdle drills inside when it was too cold or snowy outside. During these practices, I met and became good friends with more people, which made my experience at this new school that much better. The season started with indoor meets. Some of the talent that was part of that championship football team was on the track team, and it was amazing to see those athletes do so well. They made me feel welcomed and at home, and it was cool.

Tyson and Brandon continued to be my good friends, but I was getting closer to Brandon. We had more in common, and I felt more comfortable hanging out with him. My English teacher had extra tickets to a Pacers game and gave them to me, and I decided to take Brandon, whose parents brought us to the game. I didn't ask my aunt for much simply because I didn't want to be a burden to her. I don't know if she intended to make me feel that way, but I did. We went to the game, and it was so fun. At halftime, we went from the nosebleed section to the seats closer to get a better look at the court. We almost had to move from those seats but were able to stay. Our friendship blossomed into a strong one. We fought and argued, but at the end of the day, that was my bro.

One day Brandon had tickets to another Pacers game when the Lakers were in town. We both were big Lakers fans and wanted to root our team on. I had practice and didn't want to miss out, so I wanted to know if he could wait for me, but he couldn't. I tried to get a ride from my aunt but was unable. That frustrated me, which led to this next event. One of the guys on the team invited me to a minor-league baseball game downtown. I was down to go because I was getting a chance to hang out with one of the most popular dudes in the school, and it sounded like it would be fun. So I went without asking my aunt. I was now seventeen and more independent than ever.

I didn't get home until late, and when I arrived, my aunt and cousin were gone. They went back to Fort Wayne to visit without me. Many thoughts ran through my head. The first was that I was in trouble for not communicating to my aunt about my whereabouts. The second was *They freaking left me!* I knew I was in the wrong for not telling her. I was seeking attention so much and wasn't getting it for whatever reason. That was me rebelling against everything.

I decided that I had to get to a place where I could decide things for myself. I didn't know who had my best interests at heart anymore, and it was a frustrating thing. She left, and I took it to mean that she didn't care enough to make sure I was okay. As most hurt kids do when they are constantly disappointed, I went into a protective bubble and tried not to let people in, and things only got worse.

They returned home after the long weekend, and I don't remember much of a conversation about what happened, which was cool with me. My mission was to do what I was supposed to do and be away from home as much as possible. The other frustration was that I knew that our time in Indianapolis was coming to an end, but I didn't want to face that reality. Aunt Q. visited Fort Wayne so many times, and I could tell that it would be a matter of time before she told us we would be moving back. I decided to savor the moments.

Jerrell, my friend from TASS who lived near Chicago, wanted me and Dillon to come visit for his birthday. We planned to spend a couple of days there and go to a Bulls game. Kenya offered to pay for my train ticket, and I was good to go; I just needed permission from my aunt, and she would not let me go. Jerrell's parents tried to talk to her, to no avail. I couldn't understand why she wouldn't let me go, and I was so frustrated with her.

School continued to get better, and my grades improved. I brought my Spanish and chemistry grades up to a C, which was a win in my book. Track was going well. I was good enough to be on the varsity on any other team. Our team was so loaded with talent that I was forced to run on the junior varsity the whole season. We had fun anyway. It turned out to be the best season I have had since being in high school, and I was ready for the next year so I could be on the varsity and get a ring. The team went on to win the state championship, and I cheered them on the entire way.

CHAPTER 25

This Is It!

The time that I knew was coming arrived, but I didn't want to accept it. It was time for us to move back to Fort Wayne. I really tried to fight it, but Aunt Q. wasn't having it. I decided that I wasn't going down without a fight, and I was going to try to make some moves. That entire summer was Operation Get Back to Indianapolis. I was willing to do anything to get back down there, and I didn't care who was going to be hurt in the process. It was time that I got my way.

When we moved back, we returned to the home we left. I reconnected with my friends Jason and Sean, whom I had kept in touch with while I was away in Indianapolis. They became my refuge as the rift between me and my aunt grew deeper. I tried to stay away as much as possible, and it almost got me arrested.

I went over to Jason's house and ended up staying over there for several days. My original intent was to stay there just to get away, but we heard through the grapevine that another friend of ours had come up on some money by robbing rich people's houses. I wanted in on the action. The Black Expo was coming up again, and I was on track to go, but I wanted to make sure that my gear was right before I went, and I needed money to get it. Jason and I decided that we would join our other friend if he was going out to rob again. There I was, willing to ruin my future over a dumb decision, and I was going to do it because I wanted money.

I hadn't really been to church as consistently as I had when I lived with my grandma, so I don't know if you could say that I was doing my part in my relationship with God, but boy, did I feel like He never strayed away from me. We were never able to get hold of my friend, and robbing people's houses never happened, thank god. But being the young and ambitious mind that I was, had to find another way, so Jason and I walked around different neighborhoods checking people's cars to see if they were unlocked. We got into a couple of cars, but we didn't find anything of value. Once again, we made it home that night without getting caught by the police, and it was only by His grace that I didn't go down the wrong path that night—or that week for that matter.

As much as it seemed that there was divine intervention going on in my life that week, Jason and I found ourselves participating in more mischief. Someone was throwing a party from our school. Jason and I made our way to the party, much to the dismay of Sean, who was the friend who tried to keep us out of trouble.

At the party, Jason immediately started to drink the booze that was available. He was the first one to get hammered. I found comfort in a bottle of cherry vodka, which was so sweet and delicious that I almost forgot it was alcohol. That was a huge mistake. I ended up being really drunk, to the point where it was hard to focus or even walk. We both were so drunk that Sean had to babysit us. We clearly weren't in any position to go home, so we ended up staying at another friend's house, from our school, until we sobered up. His dad was rarely home, so we weren't at risk of getting caught. My head was spinning, and I told myself I would never get drunk like that again.

When I made my way back home, I found out that Aunt Q. was worried about my not coming home (I like to say she pretended to be worried), and she ended up calling the police, saying that I ran away. When I got home about five or six days later, my cousin Ashley declared that I was in trouble because they didn't know where I was, and it was a big debacle. And worst of all, my aunt contacted my mentor, and he said that I couldn't go to the Black Expo. So all that trouble was for nothing at the end of the day because my decision to stay away from home, and to possibly steal, cost me a trip to Nap all because I wanted my gear to look nice. I wasn't too upset about it. I knew that I had made a mistake, and I had to suffer the consequences.

Operation Get Back to Indianapolis hit a roadblock. I pretty much had three options, and two of them closed quickly. My great-aunts in Indianapolis didn't want me to stay with them, which I understood. My cousin Kenya had her own kids, which were already a handful, and that left me with the option of staying with my friend Brandon. His parents were going back and forth about it being fine for me to stay with them, but Aunt Q. wasn't cool with it. I wasn't about to argue, but I knew that I didn't want to stay in Fort Wayne. I was not going to budge on that because I wasn't sure that people had my best interests at heart anymore.

When I moved in with Aunt Q., I was told that adoption would happen. We were over a year and a half in, and nothing was happening, at least from my perspective. I think my aunt could see that I wasn't okay with staying in Fort Wayne anymore, so she started brewing up something that I could not even imagine.

She told me that Indianapolis was not going to happen but that California may be an option. It was something that I had not considered before. I immediately considered colleges there and got excited. They had my major that I was considering, and that was kinesiology. In my mind, California was another place that was different from my hometown, and I had family there, which was a plus. I even looked up the two possible schools I would go to in Long Beach: Anderson or Western. The more I researched the area and schools, the more excited I got about the possibility of moving to sunny Southern California.

I don't know if she knew how serious I was about making this move happen, but once it was presented to me, I started to set the wheels in motion. The next step was connecting with my family out in California. My great-grandmother, on my mother's side, who had always tried to get me to come live with her in Cali, spearheaded the movement to get me there. She persuaded her daughter, another one of my aunts, to let me stay with her for the year, and I would help her with her dog and with things around the house. She had a two-bedroom home she recently purchased, and the extra room was available for me to use. It was a perfect setup. She wanted to speak to me over the phone and see where my head was at. Her main concern was that I came to handle business and not goof around. I assured her that this was all about business. I was coming there to accomplish my goals and dreams. She believed me, and now I had a place to stay in California.

The next step was to pick the high school. I decided I would go to Long Beach Western for two reasons. First, they wore uniform. It made it easier to shop for school clothes, especially since SoCal and Indiana are two completely different parts of the United States. What was cool in Indiana might not be cool in Cali, and I didn't want to stand out if I didn't have to. Second, the track team for Anderson was loaded, and I thought I could be of more help to the Western track team than the Anderson team. Just when I thought all hope was lost and I was about to be stuck in Fort Wayne after experiencing a city so awesome in Indianapolis, I was set to move to California for my senior year of high school.

The final step was the flight, and when I asked Mr. Hayes if he could help, he wondered why I wouldn't finish my senior year and then go. I explained to him that, by going now, I would qualify for in-state tuition the next year when I went to college. He agreed that it was a good idea, and he ended up buying the plane ticket for me—a one-way trip to Los Angeles from Indianapolis. Everything was set, and I was as excited as ever. But of course, it wasn't going to be that easy.

Aunt Q. was amazed that I made so many things happen so quickly and became very pessimistic about the situation. As my departure date got closer and closer, she kept saying that it was not for sure yet. In a sense, she was right. There was a court date pending at the end of August, and in my mind, it was to let me go, but I found out that wasn't the case. I ended up going about the days as normal as possible, trying to stay under the radar, especially since I had gotten in trouble a few weeks back. Now that this plan was in motion, I didn't want to be the reason why it didn't happen.

At this point, everything was routine. I was scheduled to start school in Fort Wayne, at my old high school, before we left for Nap. They started school almost a month earlier than the one I would go to in California. When it came time for me to go to school, I wasn't doing much of anything because I knew in my mind that I was making the move to Cali. Since they hadn't started school yet, I wasn't behind and could cruise through until it was time to go. I persuaded the school to let me take a class similar to study hall or become a teacher's aide because I was just passing the time until it was time for me to move.

As much as I hated being in the system, it did have its perks, like my free health and dental insurance. I was always on top of my doctor appointments. I needed to get my wisdom teeth pulled, and I thought there was no better time to do it than at that moment. I had five that needed to get pulled—an X-ray revealed an extra wisdom tooth growing in, which surprised everyone, including my dentist. My aunt took me for my appointment, and next thing I knew, I was in la-la land. When it was done, I didn't feel anything in my mouth, and I didn't feel good. I felt queasy. When I got to the car, I threw up, and we went back in, and they said that was okay. That wasn't the worst of the pain.

We took some time to get the prescription filled that I would need for the pain, which I didn't think I needed right away, but I was wrong. As soon as that medicine from the surgery wore off, I was in so much pain. I couldn't believe how painful it was. I finally got the meds, and it was smooth sailing from there. The only other thing that sucked was that I started to look like a chipmunk. I stayed in the house for the most part, but that didn't stop people from seeing my fat face. My cousin Kevin wasn't easy on me.

Eventually, I returned to school; but at that point, I was a day or two away from court, and I was just saying my goodbyes to everyone. I said goodbye to my favorite teachers and friends, and the wait for court was the next step.

August 30, 2006, came, and my life would take a dramatic turn for the better. This court date wasn't like any other because, in my mind, something was finally going to get done. I had gone to court and hoped for change—or hoped it wouldn't be another negative update on the status of my mother. This date was for me to head off into the sunset. We walked in, and my other siblings were there—all five of us in the same room for the first time in several months. We all sat in our respective seats, and they proceeded with the normal protocol.

As the judge, caseworkers, and lawyers began to speak, I noticed that the court date wasn't about my moving; it was a freaking checkup. I am not sure why I thought that this would be a court date about allowing me to move, but I started to get nervous. My heart started to pound hard. It was beating so fast, and my hands were so sweaty. I was wondering what was going to happen and if anyone was going to tell this man that I had plans to move to another state. Not only did I have plans but I also was ready to be on a plane the next morning. This could not be happening. Everything was set up, and I refused to not stand up for myself and speak up.

As the proceedings continued, I started to gain the courage to speak up for myself, and I finally raised my hand at a break in the back-and-forth among the judge, caseworkers, and lawyers. The judge acknowledged me, and I stood up, nervous and anxious. I explained to him that I thought that this was a court date for me to finalize moving to California. I told him that I had a flight the next day and had a place to live when I got there. I also mentioned that I had plans to go there and establish residency for college. I wanted to major in kinesiology as I had developed a love for sports. I let him know that I would appreciate it if he allowed this to happen. He was shocked. He didn't know what to say at first.

As I looked around, I could see the shock on everyone else's face as well. My siblings had no idea I was planning this, so this was the first that they had heard of it. My aunt wasn't going to say anything about my plans, so she was shocked that I built up the courage to say something. The courtroom was eerily quiet as if I had done something wrong.

The judge finally broke the silence by asking if anyone could confirm my plans, and my aunt and caseworker reiterated what I said. The judge then said that he was happy I was a good student and stayed out of trouble, for the most part, and didn't see why this would be an issue. He wanted my caseworker to confirm with my aunt in California that I would move there with her, and that would be all. He also wished me well and said that, since I had been a good kid, I deserved to finally get what I wanted.

I was so excited, but it was sad as well. I was going to move to another high school—my third, the sixth school in seven years—another state, and a completely new world, yet I was so happy. How often do kids in the system get to find their happy? How often do you hear a story end with a happy ending such as this? I knew that this was something that I needed—to break the ties of my past—and I wanted it in the worst way.

As the proceedings ended, I embraced my siblings because this would be the last time I would see them for a long time. That was another reason to be sad. I hugged them and told them I loved them and that I would keep in touch.

After we left the courthouse, I had to go to school and withdraw and get my transcripts. I was officially leaving. I went home to finish packing my entire life in suitcases. My mentor brought me the plane ticket, two big suitcases, and some money to help me travel and settle in when I got to California. He wished me well, told me he loved me, and hugged me for quite a long time. I knew I was going to miss him dearly, but I had to do this; everything about the move felt so right. I finished packing, and I was ready to go.

I said goodbye to Aunt Q., Kevin, and Ashley and got in the car with my cousin Kenya, and we took our trip to Indianapolis (where I was scheduled to leave from very early the next morning), the place that started all of this—my renaissance of sorts. This place started the idea that life is bigger than what we see. There is more out there that we don't always get to experience, and once I got a taste of something better than what I was experiencing, that was it. There was no way I was going to go back to Fort Wayne, knowing that there are other places in this country with bigger and better opportunities to spread my wings and fly.

I had thoughts of what it would be like when I moved. I was a couple of months away from my eighteenth birthday, and I wondered if I would be scared to get on the plane as we sped past the cornfields. My cousin was the perfect last person I saw before embarking on this journey because she was one whom I admired for her go-getter attitude. She saw that sparkle in my eyes. She knew there was no turning back for me.

We arrived in Nap, and I didn't get much sleep. Whenever I was slated to go on a trip the next day, I rarely got any sleep because of the excitement. As the morning approached, Kenya woke me up, and I got ready to go. It was a super-early flight, but that didn't matter to me. I thanked her again, and she hugged, kissed, and wished me well.

There I was, getting ready to get on a plane for the first time ever. The whole process was such a blur, but the thing that stuck out to me was that it was gloomy and rainy out. I worried that there would be turbulence, but then I figured I had nothing to worry about since the rain wasn't that bad. As I sat in my seat, it hit me: the rain was a symbol of what my life had been like living in Indiana. It had been a storm, and it was one that came and went but mostly stayed for a while. I was about to leave the storm that was so stagnant in my life.

The pilot mentioned that we would take off shortly, and I got excited, thinking, *This is it.* The seat belt sign came on, and I was already buckled up. We started to move backward and taxi our way to the takeoff point. As the plane started to go, I felt like I was on a fast roller coaster at Cedar Point. As we lifted off, I got nervous because it was something I hadn't experienced before. This was it. I was about to be thirty thousand feet in the air, and there was no looking back. As we ascended past the clouds, the sun started to show itself as if it knew the party wasn't going to start until it arrived. Then it hit me: the sun is always shining.

CHAPTER 26

Evolution

When I arrived in California, it was as sunny as you see in the pictures and movies. It was beautiful. I couldn't help but be in awe of the amazing scenery and vibrant people. As amazing as California was when I arrived, my time here didn't come without its fair share of troubles. I was so fixated on leaving the place I called home that I failed to realize a move across the states didn't change what I had been through. The move didn't erase all the things I was struggling to push past. I harbored a lot of anger and frustration, and that led to burning bridges and alienating myself from family and friends. I struggled to trust family members and tried to deal with everything on my own.

When I moved to California with my aunt Violet, I did not get adopted. At that point, being almost eighteen and after so many failed attempts at getting something I longed for, I was content with living with my aunt. She provided me with the home I needed to progress toward my goals. She took care of me as best she could, and I adjusted to the new environment. I did my best to acclimate myself to the new school, but it was hard trying to fit in with seniors who had been there way longer than I had. It helped that I ran track because I made friends through that outlet, but if I hadn't, senior year would've been tough.

I also had a plan that I figured was foolproof: to finish high school and go to college. That kept me on the straight and narrow. I graduated from high school and had gotten into two colleges: California State University,

Northridge, and California State University, Fullerton. I was leaning toward Cal State Northridge because it was far enough where I would be leaving home, but Aunt Violet shut that down by saying it would be too far if I ever needed help. I ended up choosing Cal State Fullerton but not without resistance.

I got my first job at McDonald's a couple of months into moving to California, and I have been working a job from that point up until now. When I started my freshman year of college in the fall of 2007 at Cal State Fullerton, I was working at Target. My aunt did the best she could to help support me, but I had to pull my weight. This sense of independence caused me to clash with her, ultimately causing her to tell me to fall in line or move out. Being stubborn, I opted to move after the fall semester, and decided I would move to Tallahassee, Florida, with my best friend Brandon, from Indianapolis. His family had moved him and his little brother back to Florida after he graduated.

At this point, I made that move to get away from family and figure out things for myself without anyone meddling in my life. I was tired of being told what to do and how to do it. My frustration had reached an all-time high with everything that had happened to me; and I felt that this would be the moment I needed to finally be free from it all. When I lived in Florida, it may have been a new low. I was still trying to find myself, but things just weren't going the way I wanted them to go. I really couldn't figure it out, and I was in a serious slump. I was in Florida for a couple of months before an event happened that started my path back to California.

Brandon, his cousin, and I had rented a three-bedroom townhome together, and we all were pulling our weight to pay the rent. Brandon's parents fronted the deposit to help us get the apartment, and they felt like they still had a say in the happenings in the apartment. I didn't like that because I moved to Florida to get away from that. I was even more independent now than I was in California, holding two jobs at Circuit City and Sam's Club. I was also trying to get my schooling situated to continue my education I had started at Cal State Fullerton. Brandon's dad was an alcoholic, and that was a major trigger for me. I didn't want to be around anyone who got overtly drunk, and I didn't want to be around him when he was like that.

One day Brandon's dad came over while Brandon was at work, and he gave me and Brandon's cousin a hard time. He would come every now and then to mess with us, but on this particular day, I had enough. He was drunk as drunk could be, and I challenged him by telling him to leave us alone and stop bothering us. He flipped. He called me all types of expletives. He felt that I had disrespected him and wanted to do something about it. He picked up the nearest object he could find, and unfortunately for me, it happened to be a steel chair. He threw the chair at me and it hit me in the head.

It took every drop of restraint in me not to hurt that man. Despite the red I was seeing from rage, I convinced myself that hurting this man could lead to dire consequences. Upset, I walked out of the house and called my great-grandmother in California. She calmed me down, and from that moment, I realized I needed to make my way back to California. A couple of weeks later, I made the move back to California, much to the dismay of Brandon. Our friendship hasn't been the same since.

The Florida experience humbled me big-time. It was a move that I regretted for a long time, but it helped me start to shape myself into the man I am today. When I got back, I apologized to Aunt Violet and made things right with her. I started to reflect and accept responsibility for the things that I could control in my life. I had been through a lot, but I couldn't let that hinder my path to success. I would fall some more before I started to see a triumph, at one point suffering from mild depression. I had so many moments where I questioned internally, *Why me? Why can't I figure this thing out?*

To find those answers, I tried to find a church to go to consistently, but I found myself attending a bunch of churches that were nothing like the one I grew up in. I continued to go back and forth with attending church and missing it, until I eventually found a church home, which my wife helped me find.

How I found my wife was no fairy tale. I had committed to being a good boyfriend to whatever woman I decided to date as I had been taken advantage of in the past. I knew that if I was ever going to find the woman who was for me, I needed to commit to being the best boyfriend/husband I could be. When my wife and I started dating, I did my best to uphold that standard, but I struggled at times because I had a hard time trusting that she wouldn't hurt me like other girls. We learned a lot about ourselves and each other before we committed to marriage, and during that time, I realized she was the one I was going to be able to "do life" with.

How we met was slightly unorthodox at the time. We met online in 2008. I was browsing Myspace one day, and when I came across her profile page, I thought she was cute, and I sent her a message. She informed me that she had a boyfriend at the time but was interested in being friends. I didn't have anything to lose, and as we got to talk more, I learned that we had a lot in common. Being friends didn't sound like a bad idea at the time. We continued to talk every now and then, but after a while, we didn't talk as often.

After about a month or so without talking to each other, on Valentine's Day, I decided to contact her. I texted, "Happy Valentine's Day."

She replied, "What's so happy about it?" I realized that she probably wasn't with her boyfriend anymore, and later, she confirmed that fact. We started to talk more often, and we officially became a couple in April 2009.

We dated for four years before I proposed but not without issues. We were close to breaking up at one point, but we decided to stay together. However, a couple of months before I proposed, we did call it quits. In that moment, I thought I had lost her. I realized that I didn't want to be with anyone else but her, in spite of our disagreements. My heart was so hurt as I tried to imagine life without her. We worked it out and got back together. I proposed to her in 2013 in front of everyone at her church. In the eight years that we have been together, she has proved to me that I have made the best decision. She is my best friend, and I am happy to call her my wife and the mother of our child.

My wife started attending our current church, Experience Christian Ministries, in 2012 with her family. I was being stubborn and felt more comfortable at my own church, St. Stephen Missionary Baptist Church. She would not budge, and she urged me to attend her church because she sensed I would like it better. I started to see a change in her that I liked, and I would visit every now and then when I wasn't working on a Sunday.

At the time, I was working many jobs. Eventually, I gave in because I did prefer her church more, and we started consistently attending together in 2013. We have been loyal members since.

Attending this church has challenged my thinking as a Christian, helping me to fully understand my responsibility to Christ. There is a requirement of me to uphold certain standards, and I do not falter if I mess up. I just get back up again and keep moving in the direction that He wants and needs from me. It has challenged me to be not only the best husband I can be but also the best man.

As I got older and embarked on my own journey, one of the burdens I carried was the pressure of leading by example for my younger siblings. I felt some responsibility toward them because I essentially left them for my own selfish reasons. I made a decision for my life that turned out to be the best one I ever made, but it came at the cost of being away from my siblings and the rest of my family. It was a really tough decision to make, and I have flirted many times with going back home, but I know that I would not be where I am today had I not made the decision. Its consequences have always stuck with me.

The burdensome thought of whether I made a mistake of leaving my sister Lexus with the Williams family is still something that I have to deal with. I know that she suffered some things that I feel she will share when she is ready. I will respect her enough to wait for her to tell her story. All I can say is that I had to do what was best for me, and that ultimately led to there being a direct consequence for her. I wondered if I was there enough to support her in her time of need as I tried to "find myself" during those tumultuous times. I wondered if she would have had the childhood I thought she would if I had stayed. I don't have the answers to those thoughts, but one thing I know for sure is that everything happens for a reason. Our adversity makes us more equipped to gain our glory.

My sister Lexus will be getting married in 2018 to a man who treats her like a queen. She has three beautiful sons and is working full time. My sister Renee has two adorable little girls and is a nursing assistant. My sister Mercedes struggles every now and then with residual effects from our past, and I do my best to check in with her regularly to make sure she's on track for her life. She does the best she can, like my mother used to do before she was on drugs and in and out of jail. She's a fighter. She has a daughter and a son, both of whom were born prematurely, but they are now healthy and full of life. My brother, Luther Jr., has had his fair share of problems. He has been in and out of jail, much like his parents. My brother suffers from a couple of mental disorders and is trying to reclaim his health so he can have a peaceful, successful life. He has a personality that is wonderful, despite his upbringing, and I don't think any amount of trauma will take that away. I know he will land on his feet eventually.

I keep in contact with my mother, but I had always gone back and forth between being angry with her and not wanting to speak to her and wanting to resolve those feelings so I could have a healthy relationship with her. I mean, we went years, at one point, without speaking to each other. It is crazy to think about when you talk about mother and child, but I truly viewed my mother as a stranger. I had to forgive her and start the process of restoring our relationship, and we now speak frequently.

My relationship with my dad is stable. I harbored a lot of anger toward him for not being there enough. I blamed him often for the abuse I suffered at the hands of Luther. I just wanted him to save me, and he was never there when I needed him. We have had some deep conversations that enabled me to understand more why he wasn't there, and we are now on speaking terms.

As much as I have matured, I am not sure what I would do if I ever saw Luther, my stepdad. I have forgiven him for all he has done to me and my family, but I haven't seen him since I was in sixth or seventh grade. We don't have any relationship by any stretch of the imagination, and I am okay with that. But talk about being strong and forgiving: my sisters have invited Luther back into their lives, and they are currently trying to establish a new relationship with him. I am so proud of them. I haven't felt the need to reach out to him, but that may change down the road.

When I returned from Florida, I could not return to Cal State Fullerton, so I ended up going to Long Beach City College. I grew a lot during this time in my life. I ran track and made some lifelong friends, who ended up being in my wedding, who challenged me to continue to pursue success. It was during this time that I fell in love with poetry. I wrote poems periodically, but I never considered sharing them. I was not confident in my writing ability, but I knew that I had a story to share.

A friend from work told me about an open mic, and the rest is history. I started to entrench myself into the culture of poetry, and I became brave enough to tell my story. It was so therapeutic for me. I used to never want to share my past. I kept from people that I was a former foster youth. The open mics allowed for me to have a voice and a way to break through my frustrations. I was tutored and mentored by people who became genuine friends, and they truly helped me move past some things that held me back.

This past of mine was enough to keep most people in the doldrums of lost hope. I could've sunk into despair or fallen prey to every statistic that said I would fail. The odds were so against me. It's a wonder that I'm in the position I am today. After I received my associate degree from Long Beach City College, I went on to get my bachelor's degree in movement and sport science from the University of La Verne. I was so set on working in sports that I pursued a master's in coaching and athletic administration from Concordia University Irvine. When I was finishing up with that degree, I got an internship to work at UCLA in the Academic and Student Services Department for athletics. I worked this internship in hopes of receiving opportunities to work in other collegiate athletic departments, but that didn't come to fruition.

What did happen during the internship was that I got an opportunity to work for Pac-12 Networks. I started off as a runner (striking wires, assisting folks where needed, grabbing coffee for announcers) and worked my way up to a statistician, where I give pertinent stat information to the announcers or the people who assist with the live production. Once I learned and got better at it, more opportunities became available, and now I have done work with ESPN, Fox Sports, and other entities. I have worked at many sporting events in the last few years, including various UCLA and USC events, other college events, high school sports, NBA, MLS, and most recently NFL.

When it came time to find a job, it was about three months away from our wedding, and I was stressing about not getting an opportunity. I ended up fasting from electronics and social media for three days to clear my mind and find the answer I needed. Most people think of fasting as only going without food for a certain amount of days. But you can fast from anything that distracts you from being able to tune in to God's (or your spirit's) message. This is where the wisdom you need to make sound decisions for your life resides.

I got the answer. I needed to widen my search to more jobs that were not sports related. I came across a job for my current organization as a mentor for foster and probation youth. I am currently employed at a nonprofit, where I work with students in different capacities, including counseling and mentoring. There have been opportunities for me to go back to college athletics, but I have felt that God wanted and needed me to be in this position to help students in the way that I do. I loved this work so much that I decided to go back to get a second master's in education for school counseling at Concordia University Irvine. My hope is to become a school counselor at a middle or high school. In the future, I plan to pursue further education in counseling or therapy to expand my counseling reach outside the school confines.

I am a proud husband, father, track coach, counselor, poet, freelance sports statistician, and writer, among other things. As it stands, people wouldn't believe the things I have had to overcome to be where I am now. I think often about what kind of father I will be and whether I will falter as a husband. My son is everything I hoped he would be. He came in a flash, two weeks early, at eight pounds four ounces. When he smiles, I feel like everything I have been through was worth it. I believe I will be a damn good father because I know all too well what it is like for a boy to not have a relationship with his dad. All I want to do is be a good role model for him, and I pray I am on the right track. As a husband, I am doing great. My wife and I just celebrated our third anniversary, and I can't wait to continue to celebrate each milestone with her. She truly is my best friend.

How will I keep myself from doing the things that plagued my childhood? The answer is simple: I control the things I can control and be the best I can be, by choice, every day. My faith has carried me a long way, and as I have gotten older, it has allowed for me to worry less. I understand why troubles come our way and that it is our duty to navigate through them, not only to showcase our spiritual strength for ourselves, which builds strong self-esteem and confidence in our identity, but also to use our victories to help others along their journey. We must not live in mediocrity. Every avenue must be explored, every opportunity taken.

It took a while to realize that my story, as painful and traumatic as it was at times, has ultimately become my glory. It wasn't until my current pastor taught me, at a Bible study one evening, that we go through things so that we may be able to assist those who are currently going through the same situations. This has always stuck with me, and I believe it is my purpose to work with students whose stories closely resemble my own. I have come a long way, and I have had the opportunity to experience a lot of things. I was the student commencement speaker at my college graduation. In my job as a sports statistician, I've worked courtside at Lakers and Clippers games, often being spotted on television by friends and family. These are things I would've never thought possible—but God!

EPILOGUE

Living in Indiana, most of the days were gloomy. There were days that we were not able to see the sun. That would lead you to believe that the sun goes away, but this is not true. *The sun is always shining.* No matter what I have been through or what storm I was stuck in, the sun is eventually going to show its true colors. I left Indiana in gloom and rain, and as soon as I lifted above that, I saw the sun.

We must always allow our light to shine because the sun always lets its light shine. Things might get in the way and obstruct it, but it never stops shining. I knew then that I made the right move and that God was always looking out for me; I just needed to allow my light to shine.

The move to California didn't change the fact that life was hard; it just made it easier to challenge myself to be different. Growing up, my environment was filled with low income, living paycheck to paycheck and with government assistance, and drug and alcohol abuse. Those influences often clouded my idea of being successful. Before I met my mentor, college was the last thing I ever thought about as a kid. Think about it: I had a mother and a father who did not graduate from high school. My mom always preached about finishing grade school and high school but never college.

Our personalized success is imperative. We must find it, and we must find that light that shines within us. In life, we are dealt cards and must play the hand no matter what. We must make decisions now that will set ourselves up for a future of abundant blessings. We cannot, as I always tell students, shoot ourselves in the foot. We can't continue to harm ourselves and hinder our own opportunities. We must get out of our own way.

These are the things that I have learned as I have looked back on my life, and I want you to learn from my mistakes so that you can be successful. I pray that there is triumph in your future and that you have been blessed by this story. This has been a therapeutic process. I encourage you to write your own story. We all have gone through something, and someone out there can totally relate. You can never give them the opportunity to relate if you never share. My only hope is that my story inspires you to push past your trials and triumph over your struggles. What will you do with this life that you have been blessed with? Will you choose to create light among your darkness?